DARKER

"I reckon you're having us on. I reckon there's no such person as this Darker bloke. You talk about him all the time, but we never see him, do we? You're making it all up!"

Jonas said, "Am I?" He smiled, slow and dangerous. The blackness of his eye sockets were suddenly lit with a pale glow that gleamed brighter. "Am I?" Jonas said again, in a voice that wasn't his own. "You want the dream again, boy – the one you had last night?" The glow in his eyes was bright enough to cast shadows.

The kid whimpered, made choking noises in the back of his throat; he sank down on to his knees, trembling.

"No!" he whispered. "I didn't mean it, honest!"

"Where am I?" said Jonas.

The kid said, "Everywhere! You're everywhere, Darker!"

Have you read?

Look out for:

Point Horror
Unleashed

DARKER

Andrew Matthews

SCHOLASTIC

Scholastic Children's Books,
Commonwealth House, 1-19 New Oxford Street,
London WC1A 1NU, UK
a division of Scholastic Ltd
London ~ New York ~ Toronto ~ Sydney ~ Auckland

First published in the UK by Scholastic Ltd, 1998

ISBN 0 590 11339 9

Typeset by Cambrian Typesetters, Frimley, Camberley, Surrey
Printed by Cox and Wyman Ltd, Reading, Berks

10 9 8 7 6 5 4 3 2 1

For Penny, Patrick and Leila

1

It was late when the bus dropped Mrs Court off at the top of Cadwell Road. Normally she would have avoided being out at that time, but she had gone into town to pick up her pension, and bumped into Mrs Griffiths, an old friend that she hadn't seen for ages. Mrs Griffiths had insisted on going back to her house for a cup of tea, and then they had started gossiping, and neither of them had noticed the hours slip away.

Mrs Court hated the way that the twilight shadows made everything uncertain. It would be all too easy for her to stumble over a broken paving slab, fall and break her leg or hip. That would mean being taken to hospital, and Mrs Court was afraid of hospitals, because she knew that, all too often, people her age went in and never came out again. So she walked carefully down the road, turned the corner into Saint David's Avenue and stopped, frowning.

A little way ahead, a group of youngsters were crouched beside the garden wall of number twenty-six. At first, Mrs Court couldn't make out what they were up to; then she heard the sharp hiss of an aerosol paint spray, and indignation made her forget that she was old and frail. "You stop that, now!" she called out. "Stop it before I get the police on to you!"

Mrs Court saw the white gleam of faces turning to look at her. The youngsters stood up and slowly advanced.

There were four of them, teenage boys, all wearing the same smug smile, all walking at the same easy pace.

Mrs Court's heart pounded in alarm as the boys grouped themselves around her. "What d'you want?" she demanded.

They were still and silent.

"You keep away from me, or I'll call the police!" warned Mrs Court, unable to keep a quaver out of her voice; then her nerve broke and she shouted, "Help! Help, someone!"

One of the boys held out an aerosol can and pressed the button, splattering Mrs Court's clothes with green paint. He moved his arm in a slashing movement, the can making a snake sound, and Mrs Court felt wetness on her right cheek. "Help!" she screeched. "Somebody help me!"

All along Saint David's Avenue, people stood at their windows, watching the assault. They saw the boys walk calmly away, and Mrs Court crumple on to the pavement, sobbing and whimpering.

No one made a move to help her.

2

Nick woke up half an hour before his alarm clock went off. Mum and Dad moved about from their bedroom to the bathroom, then went downstairs into the kitchen, turning on the radio to listen to the Today programme. After a while the kitchen went quiet, the front door closed and the car started. Nick vaguely registered the sounds, but his mind was somewhere else; somewhere he didn't want to be.

He remembered Palmerstone Park in late morning sunlight: people walking dogs, kids playing on the swings and slide. Louise was beside him on the bench, pushing her long hair back behind her ears. She was wearing the necklace Nick had bought her for Christmas, and the beads glistened as she said, "I don't think we should go out with each other any more."

Nick crumbled silently. "Why not?" he said.

Louise squirmed and said, "There's nowhere for us to go except get serious."

"I though we *were* serious," said Nick.

Louise wouldn't look at him; she stared down into her lap. "I don't want to be serious, Nick," she said. "I don't want to be tied down to one person. I want to have fun."

Nick had not known that she felt tied down, or that being with him wasn't fun. He said, "You can't just—"

"Don't!" said Louise. "I feel bad enough already."

"If it makes you feel bad, don't do it."

Louise shook her head as though she had walked into a cobweb. "I have to. It wouldn't be fair to either of us to carry on the way we are," she said. "I want to go out with other people, Nick. You should, too. There are loads of better girls than me around."

"I haven't noticed them," said Nick.

A wasp, attracted by the brightness and smell of Louise's hair, buzzed in front of her face. She squealed and wrapped her arms around Nick, as if holding him would make her safe.

That was when Nick knew that he had lost her. When they had hugged before, it had been like falling down a hole in the world to their own private place. Now it didn't mean anything; the special feeling had gone. Fourteen months of closeness and trust collapsed like a slow-motion film of a factory chimney being demolished. . .

That had been three weeks ago, the day after Nick's GCSEs had finished, and everything had been grey and pointless since.

The alarm clock chirruped. Nick groaned, switched it off and hauled himself out of bed.

The post arrived at eight. There was a postcard from Dando. On the front, two girls in bikinis laughed as a wave broke over them; on the back, Dando had written: *Beach, booze and babes! Glad you're not here – I'm getting your share as well. See ya!*

Typically Dando. Nick smiled, then frowned. Bummer summer! he thought.

How much worse could it get? Louise had finished with him, Dando was in Greece, and the only summer job Nick had been able to get was working mornings and Saturdays at Bargain Books in the High Street. The wages weren't great, but with so many shops in Abernant boarded up or holding closing-down sales, Nick supposed he was lucky to have a job at all.

He left the house at eight forty-five. The road sloped steeply down, giving a view out over the derelict docks and the Bristol Channel to the hills of Somerset, like dark clouds massing on the horizon. The docks were why Abernant was there; they had been built in the 1880s to ship out coal from the collieries in the Rhondda Valley. Nick's great-grandparents had moved to Abernant to find work, and his grandparents and parents had met and married there.

No docks, no me, Nick thought.

The docks were sad now, rubble and rust, water slapping against deserted quays; a place of faded memories, like Abernant itself.

Nick turned right on to Cardigan Terrace, then left into an alley that ran down a flight of stone steps. At the entrance to the alley stood an old street lamp that burned sewer gas, day and night. It was like something from a Dickens novel, and filled Nick's imagination with the coal-haulers and crane drivers who must have passed that way to get to work. . .

The present smashed through Nick's vision of the past: on one wall of the alley, *Darker* had been sprayed in dark green paint, the stylized letters tangled together like knotted string.

Nick stopped to look. Darker? he thought. Darker than what? What's that supposed to mean? He blinked rapidly. "Get a grip, Lloyd!" he murmured. "People who stand round trying to understand graffiti are in urgent need of a life!"

Mr Protheroe had already opened the shop. He was in the back room, hunched over the keyboard of a computer, swearing to himself in Welsh, looking like a bear trying to play a toy piano. He was a huge man, broad shouldered and big-bellied, with untidy grey hair and a white beard that grew down to his chest. His attempt at transferring details of his stock from boxes of index cards on to a database was giving him much grief.

"Infernal machine," he growled when he saw Nick. "Don't tell me computers can't think, because this thing's got a mind of its own – and a sadistic sense of humour. It's just lost everything I did yesterday."

"You must have deleted it by mistake," said Nick.

Mr Protheroe scowled so deeply that his half-moon spectacles slid down his nose. "I thought these things were supposed to make life easier!" he grumbled.

"They do."

"Then why are they such a pain in the backside to use?"

"Have you looked at the manuals?" said Nick.

"Which one?" said Mr Protheroe. "I've got four. A complete Scandinavian forest must have been felled to provide the paper. If I was clever enough to understand any of them, I wouldn't need a computer in the first place."

"I could do it for you, if you like," said Nick.

"No," said Mr Protheroe. "I've got to learn how to do it myself. I refuse to be defeated by a pile of electronic junk." He stabbed at a key. There was a sound of riffling cards, and a hand of Patience dealt itself across the screen. "What the—?" gasped Mr Protheroe.

Nick said, "Mr Protheroe, why are you bothering? Your old filing system works fine, doesn't it?"

"You know that, and I know that, but the Inland Revenue man doesn't," said Mr Protheroe. "My records must be kept up to date, or else. Make us a cuppa will you, Nick? I'm gasping for the draught that cheers, but does not intoxicate."

There was a copy of the *Abernant District News* next to the tea things. Nick glanced at the headline as he filled the kettle.

VANDALS DESTROYING COMMUNITY FABRIC SAYS
LOCAL COUNCILLOR

Shouldn't take them very long, thought Nick. The town's falling apart as it is!

Nick placed a mug of tea next to Mr Protheroe's left elbow, and carried his own mug through into the shop. He had loved Bargain Books since he first discovered it when he was eleven. Books were crammed on to shelves, or stood on the floor in crooked towers. The shelves were tagged with handwritten labels that said, *Archaeology, American Literature, Fiction A-Z* – but the labels bore little relation to the contents, which had been mixed into a glorious chaos – more like a lucky dip than a book shop. It was the chaos that had always appealed to Nick. He had spent entire Saturday afternoons exploring the place, finding murder mysteries on top of fairy tales, the memoirs of First World War generals snuggling up to childcare manuals. Nick had been such a regular customer that he and Mr Protheroe had gradually come to know each other, and Nick had been impressed by Mr Protheroe's knowledge of the shop. He seemed to have a photographic memory, and knew the exact location of every book; he also appeared to have read them all. "A well educated man doesn't know all the answers, but he knows which book to look them up in!" he said. Mr Protheroe could, and often did – for no apparent reason – reel off entire pages of quotations, so that sometimes a conversation with him was like a collage of other people's words.

It was a quiet morning, like most mornings. Nick parked himself on the chair behind the counter, and leafed through *Old Abernant in Photographs*. The first pictures were of thatched cottages in leafy lanes; then pictures of the docks construction. Within two years of their completion, the population of Abernant had risen from three hundred to over twenty thousand. Nick saw streets he had known all his life, laid out as building plots. A photograph of Cardiff Road showed men in stiff collars and women wearing bonnets. It had been an exciting place then, filled with fighting-drunk sailors and what the caption politely described as *ladies of the streets.* On the opposite page was an editorial from an early edition of the *Abernant District News* which ended . . .*there are neighbourhoods into which no respectable person should venture at night without a revolver.*

Like a frontier town in the Wild West, Nick thought. Dodge City, eat your heart out.

His thoughts were interrupted as the bell above the door of the shop jangled, and a customer came in.

It was a girl in a baggy white T-shirt, blue jeans and cork-soled sandals. Her light brown hair was cut in a jaw-length bob, and her green eyes widened in surprise when she saw Nick. "Ah!" she said.

Nick said, "Good morning. Can I help you?"

The girl seemed flustered; she laughed nervously.

"I hope so," she said. "I'm looking for a book."

Airhead! thought Nick. He said, "You've come to the right place, then. Which book is it?"

"*Roswell, the First Encounter* by Sol Bryer. D'you have a copy?"

"Er . . . I'm not sure," said Nick.

Mr Protheroe's voice came from the back room. "On the floor in front of Gardening. Second stack from the left, third book down."

It was right where Mr Protheroe had said it would be. On the front of the dust-jacket was a photo of a fuzzy white blob. The title was in dripping slime letters. On the back was a picture of the author – Brillo pad hair, geek face – and the blurb began: *Have US government agencies conspired to cover up the truth about what happened at Roswell, New Mexico, in 1947?*

Probably not, thought Nick. He handed the book to the girl and her face lit up.

"Great! I'll take it."

Nick slipped the book into a brown paper bag. As he was sealing the bag with sticky-tape, the girl said, "U-um, I know you, don't I?"

"Do you?" said Nick.

"You're Nick Lloyd, aren't you?"

"That's right."

"Didn't you used to go out with Louise Davies?"

Nick winced. "Used to, yeah," he said.

The girl noticed the wince and blushed. "Sorry!" she said. She handed over the right money, grabbed the book and scuttled out of the shop.

There's no escape, Nick thought. Wherever I go, Louise will come back to haunt me.

He wished that he could fall asleep, and not wake up until the misery was over.

3

Nick finished work at one o'clock. He walked to the end of the High Street, crossed Swansea Road and passed Abernant station. At the top of Station Hill he stopped to look at the view.

On his left, beyond the docks, was Dalmore Bay, popular with day-trippers because of its sandy beach and funfair. Reflected light shimmered on the windscreens of coaches parked on what had once been railway sidings. At the bottom of the hill was Harbour Bay, almost circular, with a stone breakwater jutting across its mouth. To the right lay the long curve of Pebbly Beach, with Porthcwm Woods at its far end. As Nick looked at the woods, a cold chill made him shiver. Why does that place always give me the creeps? he thought. He had played in the woods a lot as a kid, and couldn't remember anything bad that had happened there, but the sight of it always made him shudder.

At the bottom of Station Hill was the Bay View Restaurant, which wasn't a restaurant but a snack bar, and which didn't have a view of the bay. Nick went inside, bought a coffee and a salad roll, and waited for Jonas, who was supposed to meet him there but was late, as usual.

Nick had never been able to make up his mind whether Jonas or Dando was his best mate. They had been friends since the Juniors, inseparable until Nick had started going out with Louise. Dando had been all right about Louise, ribbing Nick with Romeo and Juliet jokes, but Jonas had been sarcastic, as though he resented Nick having a girlfriend.

During the GCSEs, Dando and Nick had been worried about Jonas: he had gone in on himself and seemed more and more down after each exam. Before he left for Greece, Dando had made Nick promise to try and cheer Jonas up, which was ironic considering the way that things had turned out. Nick couldn't cheer himself up, let alone anyone else.

Maybe Jonas and I should form a band – The Depression Twins, thought Nick. Music to top yourself by.

Jonas arrived at a quarter to two, and he looked a

mess. His fair hair was screaming for shampoo, and his long, thin face was grey. He was wearing a crumpled lumberjack's shirt, scruffy jeans, battered trainers and cheap shades, which he didn't take off as he slumped into a chair opposite Nick with a heavy sigh.

"How's it going?" said Nick.

"Nowhere," said Jonas. "I slept in, got up and came here. That's my day. You?"

Nick told Jonas about Mr Protheroe and the computer, hoping it would raise a smile; it didn't.

"Nice to be able to afford a computer," Jonas said. "I can't afford a cup of coffee."

"No luck finding a job, then?"

"You must be joking. I can't even get a paper round. No bike."

"Something'll turn up eventually. Bound to."

"I doubt it," said Jonas. "I might as well stencil *LOSER* across my forehead and have done with it." A biting edge came into Jonas's voice. "How's the broken heart?"

"Still beating."

"You know Louise is going out with Geoff Myers now, don't you?"

Nick's insides filled with lead. Geoff Myers, he thought. The sixth form's resident hunk.

"Just the sort she'd go for, isn't it?" sneered Jonas. "They must spend all day trying to out-pose each other."

"I didn't know, but thanks for telling me, it's made my day," said Nick. "You're a real pal, Jonas."

Jonas shrugged. "You were bound to find out sooner or later," he said. "If you ask me, you're well shot of Louise. She's a right tart."

Nick felt a flash of anger. "No, she's not," he said.

"If you say so."

He's enjoying this, thought Nick. He stuck the knife in, now he's twisting it. He said, "What is it with you today, Jonas? Have you entered a Mr Sunshine contest or something?"

"Just telling it like it is."

There was a sourness between them; Nick tried to lose it. "How about going over the fairground?" he said. "I'll give you a thrashing at *Street Warrior*."

"Don't fancy it."

"What, then?"

Jonas paused, then said, "I want to go down to the docks."

"The docks?" said Nick. "What you going to do there, count jellyfish?"

"I went there yesterday afternoon, stayed till it got dark. If you sit still with your eyes closed, and listen, you can. . ."

"What?"

"Hear things," said Jonas. "Like voices in the water, saying stuff."

"What stuff?"

"I don't know. . ." Jonas shook his head and laughed, as though he were embarrassed. "I think all kinds of things when I'm on my own."

Nick stared. Is he joking, or flipping? he thought.

Jonas had always been a bit off the wall. Nick remembered an afternoon in the summer holidays at the end of year seven when he, Dando and Jonas had watched a horror video. Nick and Dando had fallen about laughing, but Jonas had freaked, run outside and refused to come back in until the video was switched off.

Nick said, "Hey, let's go clubbing in Cardiff tonight, Jonas. Up for it?"

"And what d'you suggest I use for money?"

"On me."

Jonas went as tight as clingfilm. "I'm not a charity case, Nick," he said. "Why don't you take your money and stick it?" He jerked himself to his feet, banging his legs against the edge of the table.

"Take it easy," said Nick. "I was only—"

But Jonas wouldn't listen. He wheeled around and stormed out of the cafe.

Nick sat gobsmacked, wondering what he'd done.

4

Nick left the café and took a stroll in the direction of Pebbly Beach, feeling the heat of the sun stinging the skin on the back of his neck. Maybe it was the temperature that had made Jonas so touchy, or maybe it was the stress of waiting for the GCSE results, or maybe Jonas just had a bad attack of hormones – who knew?

Darker, whoever or whatever it might be, appeared to be popular. Nick saw the word sprayed on a pillar box in Marine Drive, on the arch of a railway bridge and on one of the benches near the boating lake – all written in the same looping letters, the same dark green paint.

Graffiti artists like to get around, thought Nick. They're nomadic. Their ambition is to travel the world, defacing public buildings. Maybe they get together and swap holiday snaps – *Here's one I did on the wall of the Vatican.* He played with the idea to take his mind off the row with Jonas.

There was the usual blare of noise from the open-air swimming baths on the other side of the lake, and the usual gang of young kids goofing-off on the crazy-golf course. Nick climbed the wide concrete steps that led up to the promenade, and Pebbly Beach opened up before him like a broad grin.

The beach was pocked with shallow pits, as if it had been shelled. Inside the pits, people lay stretched out on towels, getting down to some serious tanning. No one was swimming because of the dangerous cross-currents, but children were playing at the water line, squealing every time a wave slopped over their feet. Out in the Bristol Channel, a small white yacht leaned in the wind.

The previous summer, Nick and Louise had spent a lot of time at Pebbly Beach; it was where Nick had first learned the difference between kissing and snogging. He walked up the promenade, the memories so strong that he began to dissolve in them.

"Hello!"

The voice made Nick jump. He turned, screwing up his eyes against the sunlight, and saw the girl who had been in the bookshop that morning. She was seated on the low wall that divided the beach from the promenade. The book she had bought lay open on her lap.

"Hello," said Nick.

He was going to walk on, but then the girl said, "Look, I'm sorry about earlier on. I didn't mean to upset you or anything, it was just. . ." she raised a finger and circled it at the side of her head, ". . .mouth open, brain not in gear, you know?"

"No worries," said Nick, almost managing to make it sound true.

"Meeting someone?" the girl said.

"No."

"Me neither. Grab a slab."

Nick hesitated.

"Go on!" said the girl. "I won't bite – not so's it leaves a scar, anyway."

Nick was stuck: he didn't really want company, but he didn't want to offend the girl either. He sat down next to her and nodded at the book. "Any good?"

"A-mazing!" the girl said. "According to this bloke, right, a UFO crashed in New Mexico in 1947, and the bodies of six extraterrestrials were recovered. Only, the US military lied about it. They made out it was a weather balloon, not a UFO, and the bodies were test-dummies – but why would they put test-dummies in a weather balloon?"

"You're into all that, are you?"

"Certainly am," said the girl. "UFOs, alien abductions, paranormal activity—"

"And let me guess," said Nick. "You've got the hots for David Duchovny."

The girl nodded enthusiastically.

"'Fraid so," she said. "When he got married, it was the most tragic day of my life. How about you?"

"Can't say I fancy him at all," said Nick.

"No, I mean are you interested in the Unexplained?"

Nick shrugged. "Haven't really thought about it," he said.

"D'you do social education at the boys' comp?"

The question took Nick by surprise.

"Um, yeah," he said. "We learn about sexual perversion and how to take drugs."

"We discuss stuff like abortion and the arms trade," said the girl. "Only they're not discussions, because everybody's made their minds up before they start. If we talked about UFOs, it would be much better. People don't know what they think about them."

"Maybe the staff of the girls' comp won't let you talk about UFOs because they're part of the conspiracy to cover them up," said Nick.

"Well, the Head's an alien for a start!" the girl said. "Her dress sense is not of this earth!"

Nick laughed. He couldn't remember the last time something had made him laugh, and it felt odd.

The girl smiled at him. "I'm Carys, by the way," she said. "Carys Bevan."

"Hello, Carys Bevan," said Nick.

"Hello, Nick Lloyd," said Carys. "You could do with cheering up."

"Could I?"

"Uh-huh. You've got a big black cloud hanging over you, and it's Louise Davies shaped."

"And waiting for GCSE results shaped," said Nick.

Carys held her index fingers together in a cross.

"No, no, no!" she said. "So-rry! Not allowed to talk about GCSEs. I've declared myself a GCSE-free zone, so you'll have to think of another topic of conversation. I'll give you ten seconds, starting . . . now!"

"So tell me about Roswell," said Nick.

And Carys did – in exhaustive detail.

Nick listened, said, "Yeah?" and "Get away!" in the right places, all the time a part of him thinking, What am I doing here, listening to this girl bang on about aliens and the FBI? But a bigger part of him was fascinated – not by what Carys had to say, but by the way in which she said it.

Carys didn't just use her voice to talk, she used her whole body: wiggling her shoulders, waving her hands, hugging her knees. Her face was constantly moving; she had so many expressions that Nick thought it would be impossible to take a good photograph of her, because she was always changing.

Carys stopped in mid-sentence and clapped a hand to her forehead. "Oh n-o-o!" she wailed. "Help! I'm doing it again!"

"What?" said Nick.

"Talking too much! All my friends tell me I talk too much. They call me Em. That's short for MM – you know, Motor Mouth." She peered at Nick, tilting her head from side to side. "You've still got ears, then?" she said. "I thought I might have worn them down to stubs."

"I'm fine," said Nick. "Carry on, you've got me interested now."

"You're just saying that to be polite."

"No, I'm not."

"You must be bored. I'm surprised your buns haven't dropped off."

"I'm not bored!" said Nick.

"Now we're having an argument, and I've only known you twenty minutes!" said Carys. "I've got this thing about putting people's backs up. It happens all the time. Then I apologize too much. Sorry!"

Nick frowned. "Was that a joke, or are you serious?" he said.

"I wish I knew!" said Carys. "I don't usually get jokey or serious – just ignored."

Nick found that hard to believe, but didn't say so.

"Becky, Cat and Jools don't help much either," Carys went on.

"Who are they?"

"My mates," Carys said glumly. "Becky's a Kate Moss lookalike, Cat looks like she's stepped off the set of Baywatch and Jools is just plain, old-fashioned gorgeous. Like, if we go out together – ZAP! Hunks drop out of the sky like rain. I end up in a corner, on my own, or talking to Mr Handsome's nerdy friend." She sighed heavily. "It's called having low self-esteem, isn't it?"

Nick didn't hear the question, because suddenly the light seemed to turn into glass, and everything went strange. It was like watching a film he had seen before. He slowly turned his head to the right, knowing what he was going to see without understanding how he knew it.

The boys who had been playing crazy golf had gathered around the attendant's hut. One of the boys raised a golf club above his head and then brought it down, shattering the hut's side window. The attendant charged out, but the boys had already scattered in all directions, laughing and calling out swearwords. Passers-by froze, staring open-mouthed.

The world came back to normal.

Carys said, "Did you see that? Did you see what that kid just did?"

"Yes," said Nick.

"He just – in broad daylight! He couldn't have been more than eight or nine."

"No," Nick said.

Carys registered the flatness in Nick's voice and stared at him. "Hey, you OK, Nick?" she said.

"Yeah," said Nick, forcing a smile.

But he wasn't OK. He had felt something as he watched the boys, an invisible presence that had touched him, and made him turn his head to look.

And it was familiar; somewhere, some time, Nick had felt it before.

5

Jonas walked slowly along the road that ran through the docks, past a patchwork of foundations and rubble piles that were all that was left of railway sheds and warehouses. Except for the lapping of water against the stone blocks of the empty mooring bays, everything was silent. In the tangle of dry grass and weeds at the side of the road, rusty railway lines fanned out to nowhere.

Jonas reached an iron bridge and climbed the steps to the top, grit cracking and scraping under the soles of his trainers. At the top of the steps, he looked out over the remains of Number One Dock. Emptiness crept into him, and he began to drift into the nothing. No need to worry about money here, or friends, or relationships – none of that mattered. There was only the sound of the water, and the shift of the breeze on his face.

Jonas closed his eyes.

The voice came immediately, clearer than it had been before, as though something had given it strength.

You came back, boy.

"You knew I would," Jonas answered softly.

You're not afraid, then?

"No. Why should I be?"

Because I might not be real.

"You're real," said Jonas. "You're the only thing that *is* real."

A chuckle merged with the lapping water.

And was last night real, boy? How did you feel when that old woman cried?

"You already know. I could feel you knowing while it happened."

Are you ready for more?

"Yes. Tell me what to do. I'll do anything."

Fine words, boy, but can I be sure that you mean them?

"Yes."

Do you remember what I told you?

"Yes."

Then what's my name?

The voice was teasing, testing.

"Darker," said Jonas.

Where did I come from?

"Nowhere. You've always been and you always will be."

And where am I?

"Everywhere."

Open your eyes, boy, and see what I've brought you.

Jonas blinked against the dazzling sunshine, turned his head and looked down.

At the foot of the steps stood a group of boys, some Jonas's age, some younger. They were gazing up at him, waiting.

6

People began to drift away from the beach and the swimming baths. Children, reluctant to leave the sunshine and water, dragged their feet as they trailed along behind their parents.

Nick looked at his watch. "Time I was heading back," he said.

"You going up Lake Road?" said Carys.

"Yes."

"I'll walk with you as far as the bus stop."

Lake Road was giving back all the heat from the sun that it had stored during the day. Warmth from the pavement came through the soles of Nick's trainers, and melted tar glistened on the road.

Nick said, "What's the name for that thing you get when you feel like something's happened before?"

"Déjà vu," said Carys. "Why?"

"I got it really strongly when I saw that kid break the window," Nick said.

"A-a-h!" Carys said knowingly. "So you had an out-of-time experience!"

"My science teacher said déjà vu had something to do with blood supply to the brain."

Carys wrinkled up her nose. "He would!" she snorted. "He's a science teacher, isn't he? Scientists believe in logic."

"Don't you?"

"I believe in keeping an open mind," said Carys. "The universe is probably a whole lot weirder than you think."

"To be honest with you, I don't spend a lot of time thinking about the universe," said Nick.

Carys said, "Well, you ought to – you live there."

They reached the bus stop, and Nick felt awkward: he wasn't sure how to say goodbye.

"Thanks for the chat," he said. "I enjoyed it."

"Me, too."

"I'm glad we met up. I was feeling a bit. . ."

"I know," said Carys.

"Er . . . I expect I'll see you around, then."

"See you."

Nick walked away, thinking, Strange afternoon! Carys is so . . . so. . . He couldn't find the right adjective to finish the sentence until a bus passed him on Marine Drive. Carys was sitting next to a window, smiling and waving. Nick caught the smile and returned it. Wild, he thought. She's really wild.

But she wasn't Louise.

Mum and Dad came in from work just as the early evening news started. Dad looked into the front room and said, "OK, Mr Couch Potato, butt off cushions, into shed! Bar-b!" Then he went upstairs to change out of the suit and tie that he called his "Mr Lloyd outfit".

Nick went through into the kitchen. Mum was taking sausages and corncobs out of the fridge.

"Have we got any of that smoky barbecue sauce left?" she said.

"Top shelf, at the back on the right," said Nick. "A load of letters came for you this morning. I left them on the hall table."

"I saw them," Mum said. "They'll be the answers to the letters I sent out about the class reunion. I must have been mad when I said I'd organize it. Never volunteer for anything!"

Nick smiled, because Mum was always volunteering for things. She was a governor of Nick's school, convener of the local Neighbourhood Watch and secretary of the Abernant Women's Judo Club. Mum said she liked to do her bit for the community; Dad said she was a closet control-freak.

The back garden of the house had been paved

over by a previous occupant, but it still looked like a garden because Mum had filled it with pots, tubs and troughs of plants. Nick wheeled the barbecue out of the garden shed, lined it with baking foil and built a mound of charcoal and fire-lighters.

Dad came out of the house. He was wearing a T-shirt, shorts and flip-flops, and carrying a box of long matches. He lit the fire-lighters and watched as flames curled through the gaps in the charcoal.

"Think that's enough?" he said.

"Should be plenty," said Nick. He was watching the flames too, hypnotized by the way they flickered like beckoning fingers.

"What is it with men and fires?" Mum called from the kitchen.

"Primitive instinct," said Dad.

"All right, Tarzan," said Mum. "You can come and give me a hand with these sausages, unless you'd rather go out hunting caribou with a bow and arrow!"

"Women!" Dad said softly.

"Sexist!" said Nick.

"Your mother, then," Dad said.

Dinner smelled and tasted of summer. Seagulls yawped overhead, and there was the faint see-sawing of a police siren.

"What was your day like?" Mum ask Nick.

Nick talked about what had happened at the crazy-golf course.

Dad humphed. "It's happening all over," he said. "One of the blokes in the office lives on the Valedown estate. He's been burgled twice since the schools broke up. The police know who's doing it, but they can't prove anything. They told him it was a gang of kids, and the oldest is only fourteen. Fourteen!" Dad sighed and shook his head. "What's got into these kids?"

"Not like your day, is it?" said Mum. "Teenagers were quiet and law-abiding then. All chapel, Boy Scouts and crochet work."

Dad pulled a face and rubbed at the tattoo on his left forearm – a heart with a dagger through it, drops of blood dripping from the blade.

Nick guessed that Dad had been a bit of a tearaway in his young days. As well as the tattoo, Dad had a long scar on his right shin, a souvenir of a motorbike accident when he was nineteen. He had been married before, but he never talked about it. Nick knew because one day he had been playing about in the loft, and came across a photograph album that contained a picture of Dad with shoulder-length hair. Dad was dressed in biker-leathers, and had his arm around a dark-haired girl who wore so much mascara her eyes looked like sooty holes. Nick showed the photo to Mum, and all that Mum would say was that the girl's name was Julie, and that she had been Dad's first wife.

Nick had never asked Dad about Julie – partly

because he was afraid to, and partly because, in a way, it was exciting to have a father with a secret life.

Dad surveyed the ruins of the meal and said, "Bags I do the washing-up! Anything good on the box tonight?"

"Dream on!" said Mum. "If it's not cops or cookery, it's repeats. They do so many repeats, it's like being stuck in a time-warp! Anyway, I won't be watching anything. I've got all those letters to sort through."

"Ha!" said Dad. "And you're complaining about time-warps on telly! I don't know why you're so keen on this reunion lark. I wouldn't fancy a reunion with the people in my year at school."

"You'd have to hold it in Cardiff nick!" Mum said sharply. "My year's coming up to the Big Four-O. Getting nostalgic."

"You don't get proper nostalgia these days," said Dad. "Not like when I turned forty. Nostalgia really *was* nostalgia then."

Mum leaned over and punched him on the arm.

Nick had had the nightmare before, but not for a long time. He was a little boy, running down a path that was lined with trees, trying to escape from something, but unable to because it was inside him, a shadowy voice that filled his mind.

No use running, boy. I'm everywhere you go.

The path kept repeating itself: Nick passed the same trees, the same nettles and brambles, over and over again. No matter how hard he ran, he always ended up back where he had started.

I'm everywhere. . .

The voice was smug, mocking – a bully's voice. It made Nick feel helpless. He would have to stop running soon; when he did, the thing in his head would take him over, and then—

Nick opened his eyes to the darkness of his bedroom. He had kicked the duvet on to the floor, and the pillow beneath his head was damp with sweat.

Only a dream, he thought, but what was *only* about dreams? When you were in them, they were real; messages passed between your eyes and your brain, so you actually saw what was in the dream – another world that only showed itself when you were asleep.

Nick lay still, waiting for his breathing and heartbeat to slow down. The bedroom window was half-open, and he heard noises from the street outside: whispers, stifled giggles, the squeaking of metal on metal.

Nick glanced at his alarm clock: 01:15. Who was up and about at this time of night? He rolled out of bed, stepped to the window, opened a narrow gap in the curtains and looked out.

Something was moving at the edge of a patch of lamplight on the opposite side of the street. Nick saw a group of shadowy figures standing beside a car. They were doing something to the passenger window – Nick couldn't see exactly what – but he suddenly had the same feeling he had experienced at Pebbly Beach.

This isn't déjà vu, Nick thought. This is fear. He pushed the window wide open and shouted, "Hoi, you lot! Get away from that car!"

The figures broke into a run, feet dapping on the pavement as they went down the hill. Just before they vanished from view, one of the group half turned in a pool of lamplight, and Nick got a cold shock of recognition. "No," he whispered. "It couldn't have been."

Nick slipped on his dressing gown and slippers and left the bedroom. Dad was out on the landing. He had turned on the light, and was blinking blearily. "What's up?" he said.

"Someone was trying to break into Mr Thomas's car," said Nick.

Dad came fully awake. "Better take a look," he said.

Several neighbours had been woken by Nick's shout. Some leaned from their bedroom windows, other lurked behind their net curtains.

Mr Thomas was crouched beside his car. The window of the passenger door was open a few centimetres and the rubber seal hung down like a strand of black spaghetti.

"What's the damage, Huw?" said Dad.

"Look at that!" Mr Thomas said, pointing. On the bonnet of the car, someone had scratched *Darker* so deeply that the underlying metal gleamed through the paint. "You didn't see who did it, did you?" said Mr Thomas.

"Gang of kids," said Nick.

"Bloody kids!" Mr Thomas growled. "They want a damned good hiding if you asks me. It's getting ridiculous, mun! Why don't the police do something about it? Did you know any of them?"

"No," said Nick: but it was a lie, because he thought he had seen Jonas. What's going on here? he thought. What's happening in this town?

7

Next morning, with the sun shining down from the cloudless blue sky, Nick wasn't so sure about what he had seen the night before. You've known Jonas half your life, he thought as he went through the alley on his way to work. Sure, he can be moody and awkward – but a vandal? Nah! Must have been your eyes playing tricks on you. There's nothing going on in Abernant. Nothing ever does. It's not so much sleepy as comatose.

Nick passed a building that had once been a church. Now it was a warehouse that sold cheap tack, like life-sized plaster herons, and fruit-shaped plastic salt and pepper pots – stuff that it was sad to think of people wanting to buy. Then a stationer's and printer's shop, where the items on display in the window were faded and covered in a thin layer of dust. Then an estate agent's that had been shut for over a year. There was a mound of envelopes piled on the floor beneath the letter-box, and a bottle of long-curdled milk stood on a window ledge. Nick could almost hear the street decaying, the decay seeping into him, dragging him down.

Mr Protheroe didn't seem very down. He was flicking a rainbow-striped furry duster over the shelves, whistling loudly.

"You sound happy," said Nick. "Ticket come up on the Lottery?"

"As good as," Mr Protheroe said. "Chap came in after you left yesterday, with a bagful of books that he'd rescued from a skip. Rubbish, most of it, but one turned out to be a little treasure." He went into the back room and returned with a thin black book.

"Have a look, but handle with care," he said.

The book didn't seem like anything to get in a lather about. The title page was printed in plain black type, the letters as straight-edged as skyscrapers.

FOLK TALES & BALLADS OF GLAMORGAN
collected and translated from the Welsh
by
Reverend Aspasia Greatorex
Cardiff 1847

"Aspasia Greatorex?" said Nick. "There's a name to get stuck with! Sounds like a breakfast cereal."

"Quite a celebrity was old Aspasia," Mr Protheroe said. "Antiquarian, amateur archaeologist and an advocate of what used to be called Muscular Christianity. Won a medal for boxing when he was at Cambridge. He published a survey of ancient sites in Glamorgan, but that book's rarer. Treat it with respect – that's your heritage you're holding."

Nick gave the book back to Mr Protheroe, and stifled a yawn.

"What's wrong with you this morning?" said Mr Protheroe. "You have a somewhat wan and wistful look."

"Bad night," said Nick. "I got woken up at one o'clock by some kids trying to pinch a neighbour's car."

Mr Protheroe pursed his lips. " 'For now, these hot days, is the mad blood stirring,' " he said.

"Sorry?"

"*Romeo and Juliet*, act three, scene one," said Mr Protheroe. "A story of love, violence and the insanity of youth. Knew a thing or two about life, did Shakespeare."

"I wish I did," said Nick.

By lunchtime the shop was like a steamy bathroom, and Nick was glad to get outside. He took a deep breath of relatively cool air . . . and saw Carys looking in the window of the record shop that was two doors down from Bargain Books. She was wearing a white top and black exercise shorts under a short orange skirt. Nick went to join her at the window.

"Hello there!" he said. "Quite a coincidence, bumping into you."

"Not really," said Carys. "I've been waiting for you for the last fifteen minutes."

"Why's that, then?" said Nick, thinking that something must be wrong.

"Because I've been thinking."

"What about?"

"You, me, life, the summer," Carys said. "What are you doing?"

"When?"

"Right now."

"Er . . . talking to you?"

"Aw, give me a break will you, Nick?" Carys groaned. "Leave me some pride, eh?"

"How?"

"You eat cheese?"

"Yes."

"Good, because I've made some sandwiches. Cheese, mango chutney and mayonnaise. We're going to have lunch together in Meadow Park."

"Is that an invitation or an order?" said Nick.

"An order," Carys said. "I thought about trying the subtle approach, but with you there's no point, is there?"

Meadow Park was just off Marine Drive. The National Eisteddfod had been held there in the 1960s, and the council had constructed a stone circle for the occasion. Carys walked across the grass and sat in the shadow of one of the stones. Nick sat beside her.

The sandwiches had gone soggy, but they tasted all right. Nick and Carys drank Diet Coke from cans that fizzed everywhere when they popped the ring-pulls.

Nick spotted *Darker* sprayed on one of the stones.

"What's all that about?" he said.

Carys followed his gaze. "Search me," she said. Her face went serious. "Oops! I knew that Coke would be a mistake."

"Why?"

"Burp alert!"

"Feel free," said Nick. "I'll pretend not to notice."

Carys's belch went circling round the stones like the love-call of the world's biggest bullfrog. Nick decided that Mr Protheroe would have described it as "an effusive eructation".

"Good one!" he said. "Eleven point five on the Richter scale."

"The Richter scale only goes up to ten," said Carys. "I've ruined it, haven't I?"

"What?"

"You and me, here together," Carys said. "It

was supposed to be – I mean, I was going to tell you—"

"Carys," said Nick, "if you've got something to say, why don't you just say it?"

Carys took a deep breath. "It goes like this," she said. "You're lonely, I'm lonely – right? I thought that if we started hanging out, we could put the two lonelinesses together and they might cancel each other out. Nothing complicated, just two friends having a laugh."

Nick frowned.

"You remember laughing, don't you, Nick?" said Carys. "That thing you used to do when you were happy?"

Nick said, "But . . . if people saw us together, they'd think that we were an item, or something."

"The best way to deal with that is not to give a stuff about what people think," Carys said. Her shoulders crumpled. "But if you don't want to, that's OK. Forget I said anything."

"No!" said Nick. "It's not that I don't want to—"

"Then you *do* want to?"

Nick chose his words carefully. "I wouldn't mind if we hung out together," he said.

"Then let's do it tonight!" said Carys. "*Alien Skies* is on at the Royal and I'm gagging to see it." She stuck out her hand. "Put it there, mate!" she said.

As Nick took Carys's hand, he saw a darkness sweep over her face, like the shadow of a passing bird. The air was heavy with menace.

Cut it out! Nick told himself. You're getting paranoid in your old age.

Carys let go of Nick's hand and grinned. "You've got a big blob of mayonnaise on your chin," she said.

8

Toiling up the hill towards his house, Nick started to wonder if he had done the right thing agreeing to go out with Carys, but the heat made his mind as blank as the paving stones beneath his feet. He concentrated on the shower he was going to take as soon as he got in, then he planned to tune his bedroom radio in to a talk channel and doze. More than anything he needed some sleep; instead, he got Jonas.

Jonas was seated on the low wall outside Nick's house, wearing the same outfit as the previous afternoon and a pair of headphones attached to a Walkman in the breast pocket of his shirt. He was nodding his head in time to the music he was listening to, and it made reflected light flash off the lenses of his shades.

Nick sat down next to Jonas. "What you listening to?" he said.

"Plutonium Dwarf's new album," said Jonas. He spoke too loudly, the way people did when they were listening on headphones.

"I thought you didn't like Heavy Metal."

"So it's a crime to change my mind?" Jonas said. He slid the headphones down on to his neck and reached into his pocket to turn off the Walkman.

There was an awkward silence.

Nick said, "Coming in for a drink?"

"Not just yet," said Jonas, "Look, Nick, about yesterday afternoon—"

"Forget it."

"Must have been the heat or something. It really does my head in, you know? I haven't been sleeping too well recently and . . . I lost the plot."

"Don't worry about it. It's results pressure. We're all suffering from it."

"Yeah?" said Jonas. "You seem to be handling it OK."

"Don't you believe it," Nick said with a laugh. "Deep down inside, I'm climbing the walls."

Jonas chewed the inside of his lip. "Nick," he said cautiously, "are you having dreams? Like nightmares?"

"Off and on."

"I get them every night," said Jonas. "I shout

myself awake, and then I can't remember what I was dreaming about. Freaky."

"Don't let it get to you," Nick said.

"What?"

"The exams. My mum says being optimistic or pessimistic makes no difference to the results you'll get, but if you're optimistic you'll have a better time waiting."

"I don't think I care one way or the other any more," said Jonas. "Exams, school and all that – waste of time really."

Nick thought, Hang on, this is *Jonas* talking. Jonas who worked his butt off during study leave and got As and Bs for his mocks. He wished Jonas would take off the shades and show his eyes, so that Nick could tell if he were joking or not.

Jonas said, "I'm meeting up with some people I've been knocking about with later. Why don't you come with me? I'm sure you'd get on with them. Great laugh."

"Which people?"

Jonas shrugged. "Billy Tapscott. John Trevors."

"John Trevors?" said Nick. "He's an animal, Jonas! He makes the thing in *Alien* look like one of the Teletubbies."

"He's not as bad as he's made out," said Jonas. "Not when you get to know him. I reckon it'd do you good to come out with us."

"It would?"

Jonas's voice was soft, almost dreamy. "You'd be amazed what goes on in Abernant at night, Nick," he said. "It really comes comes alive, if you know the right places to look. You can see things that you can't see in the daytime."

Nick laughed to make it sound like a joke, and said, "You weren't round here last night by any chance, were you? Only a neighbour had a bit of bother with some lads. I saw them run off. One of them looked a bit like you."

"Yeah?" said Jonas. "Couldn't have been me, though. I watched telly all evening, then had an early night."

It came out just a bit too slick and pat, and Nick frowned.

Jonas noticed the frown, and said, "You can ring my mum and ask her, if you don't believe me. She'll tell you!"

"Calm down, Jonas! Course I believe you, you're my mate," Nick said. "I didn't say it *was* you, I said it looked a bit like you, that's all."

Jonas's face lost its offended look. "So what about tonight?" he said. "You up for it, or what?"

"Sorry. I've got something else arranged for tonight."

"With Carys Bevan?" said Jonas.

Nick was so astonished that he felt the sweat on his back run cold. "How did you know about—?"

"Saw you talking to her in the High Street this afternoon," said Jonas. "I was on my way to see you in the shop, but you looked like you didn't want to be interrupted."

"It's not like that," said Nick. "We're just—"

Jonas said, "You want to watch your step with her, Nick. She's bad news. She's supposed to be a bit. . ." Jonas tapped the side of head with his index finger. "A couple of tents short of a Boy Scouts' camp, you know?"

Nick couldn't believe what he was hearing. He said, "Thanks for the warning, Jonas, but I think I can handle it."

"Just passing on what I've heard," Jonas said. He pushed himself up off the wall and slipped the headphones back on. "You sure about tonight?" he said.

"Positive."

"You don't know what you're missing, Nick."

As Jonas walked away, Nick thought, Something's not right with him. He didn't sound like himself. Is he doing drugs, or what?

He rejected the thought as soon as it occurred to him. Jonas couldn't afford to buy drugs; but if it wasn't drugs, what was it?

Over dinner, Nick chose his moment carefully, and said, "I'm going to see that film at the Royal tonight."

"I thought you didn't like going to the cinema on your own?" said Dad.

Nick said, "I don't. I'm going with a friend."

"Jonas?" said Mum.

"No, another friend."

Dad looked at Mum, Mum looked at Nick and raised her eyebrows. "Oh?" she said.

"All right, all right, yes, it's a girl!" said Nick. "Her name's Carys Bevan. But she's a *friend*."

"I didn't say she wasn't," said Mum.

"No big romance, right?" said Nick. "I've had it with all that."

"Remind you of anyone you know?" Mum asked Dad.

Dad looked sheepish. "You'll learn, son," he said.

"Learn what?"

Dad said, "I'm not telling. Life's like a whodunnit, much more fun when you don't know how it turns out."

"What are you on, Dad – Prozac?" said Nick.

"What's she like?" said Mum.

"Who?"

"Carys Bevan."

"Horrible!" said Nick. "A loud-mouth, tarty crack-head!"

Mum held up her hands. "OK! Sorry I asked!"

"She's fun," said Nick.

Mum and Dad both went, "A-a-h!"

"What does that mean?" said Nick.

Dad said, "You'll learn, son."

Nick waited for Carys at the bus stop at the side of the town hall – the same place he used to wait for Louise. He was jumpy, and there was a restlessness in the air, a pressure that wouldn't let up. An accident looking for somewhere to happen, thought Nick.

His mind cleared as the bus pulled up and Carys stepped off. She looked different, more vulnerable than she had been in Meadow Park. Her smile wobbled at the corners. "You didn't stand me up, then," she said.

"Were you expecting me to?"

"I was afraid you might. It wouldn't have been the first time I've been stood up. I don't have any luck with boys." Carys pointed at her mouth. "My big gob frightens them off."

"You haven't frightened me off," said Nick.

"Nick Lloyd, Man of Steel!"

"Ears of steel, anyway."

They began to walk along Cardiff Road, towards the cinema.

"*Do* I talk too much?" said Carys. "I can't help it. If I think something, I've got to say it."

Nick said, "I like the way you talk. You care about things."

"Yeah, but only crazy stuff, like UFOs and the supernatural."

"Most people in this town don't care about anything," said Nick. "They're brain-dead."

"And what do you care about?"

"Pass!"

"D'you want to do A-levels and go to university?"

"If I'm good enough," said Nick. "I want to do history."

"Why history?"

"It's interesting," said Nick. "It's where we come from. You can only understand the present by looking at the past."

"I want to do languages," Carys said. "Then I can go to Europe and be an interpreter. Anything to get out of Abernant. This place died years ago, only they forgot to bury it."

Nick laughed. "You just read my mind," he said.

They looked at each other in a moment of togetherness.

Nick said, "So, what's the film about?"

"Where have you been?" said Carys. "*Alien Skies* is this summer's gotta-see movie! The hype started in March."

"Missed it," Nick said. "I seem to've spent most of this year on Planet Revision."

"Don't!" said Carys. "If you mention anything else to do with GCSEs, I'll turn into a pumpkin."

Alien Skies was a sequence of clichés lifted from

every sci-fi and action film that Nick had seen, and the plot was aimed at people who moved their lips when they read comic strips. Carys really got into it: when the first alien exploded into green mush, she jerked in her seat and grabbed Nick's hand, then pulled away as though his skin were red hot.

An actor dressed as a USAF colonel was making a speech about Freedom and Democracy, which Nick presumed meant that the aliens were going to get wiped out.

They were, by fifteen million dollars' worth of computer magic.

Nick and Carys left the Royal at nine-forty.

"And now what?" Carys said.

"What time have you got to be back?"

"No later than half-ten, or Mum and Dad turn into the Parents From Hell."

Nick looked around, thinking. The fairground and the cafés along the esplanade at Dalmore Bay would still be in full swing, otherwise there was nothing: Abernant was shut. Louise would have dragged him off somewhere dark and quiet for an hour's heavy smooching and—

"Stop comparing me with her," said Carys.

"Hey?"

"Stop comparing me with Louise," Carys said. "I can tell when you're thinking about her, because your eyes go like a spaniel's." She stepped closer and looked into Nick's face. "This is me, Nick," she said. "Undivided attention, right?"

"Sorry!"

"I can't use your sorrow, Nick," said Carys. "It's your co-operation I'm after."

They walked slowly in the direction of the town hall. Carys talked about the film, beginning most of the sentences with, "What about that bit where. . .?"

Cardiff Road was shadows and streetlight. The headlamps of passing cars flashed in shop windows.

"I wish it would rain and clear the air!" said Carys. "It feels really weird tonight, doesn't it? Like—"

From somewhere up ahead came the unmistakable sound of plate-glass breaking, followed by the wail of an electronic alarm.

Carys said, "Oh, wh-a-a-t?"

Pounding footsteps. Figures running towards them, out of the light, into the darkness and back into the light again. A gang of boys with boxes under their arms, bulging plastic bags in their hands. Two boys ran into the gutter to avoid Nick, a third collided with him. Nick seized the boy's shoulders and swung him round.

"Get off me!" the boy shouted. "Get off!"

"What the hell d'you think you're doing?" said Nick.

The boy was small – aged nine or ten, Nick thought. His face was clenched and angry. "If you don't get off me, Darker'll get you!" he gasped.

"What?" said Nick.

"Darker'll have you!" the boy snarled. "He'll have you – easy!" Something in his eyes moved like ink in water.

Whatever had been with the kids at Pebbly Beach, and around Mr Thomas's car, was here. A cold prickle went from between Nick's shoulder blades to the back of his neck. He felt himself shrinking into a frightened child. "Who's Darker?" he said.

A hard voice came from behind. "Better let him go, pal."

Nick turned, and saw a bigger boy. His face was pale, almost silvery. He had the same look in his eyes as the boy Nick was holding. Nick thought he recognized him from school, but he couldn't remember his name.

"What's it to you?" Carys demanded angrily.

"Stay out of it, love," the boy said.

"I'm not your love!" Carys snapped.

Nick's fingers relaxed. The small boy tore himself free and ran. The bigger boy gazed at Nick without flinching. He had a pebble the size of a cricket ball in his right hand.

In a dry whisper, Nick said, "Who's Darker?"

The boy sniggered. "If you got to ask who Darker is, you wouldn't understand me if I told you," he said. He drew back his right arm, and everything went into slow motion.

Nick heard Carys shout, "Watch out!" — saw his arm come up to push her out of the way, saw the pebble leave the boy's hand and get bigger as it flew towards his face. Then Nick dived; the pavement sailed up at him, and he felt the jolt of his body hitting the concrete.

The boy vaulted over Nick and charged down Cardiff Road, swerving left at the corner of Deacon Street.

Carys leaned over and put her hand on Nick's arm. "Nick?" she said.

"I'm all right," said Nick.

Carys helped him to his feet. They were both trembling.

"I thought he was going to kill you!" said Carys. "Did you see the look in his eyes?"

"Must've been spaced out," said Nick.

On the morning that he first met Carys, Nick had wondered how the summer could possibly get any worse. Now he knew.

9

Halfway down Deacon Street, Billy Tapscott stopped running. He stuffed his hands in the pockets of his baseball jacket and strolled to the junction with Dock Road. He had nothing incriminating on him – Billy wasn't mug enough to get caught in possession of stolen property – and if the police picked him up, he would be able to bluff his way out of it. Anyway, Billy wasn't really interested in stealing. Seeing the shop window disintegrate and hearing the alarms sound had made him feel excited, alive. It was a better high than booze or blow, because when you were on, everything got fuzzy and mixed up; now he was sharp, kicking.

Billy turned left on to Dock Road, walked past

the lights in the windows of the Castle Arms, glanced around to make sure that nobody was about, climbed over an iron railing, and scrambled down the steep slope that led to the disused railway lines of Number One Dock. The darkness was no problem. Billy's night eyes were like a cat's. He could make out the railway bridge, and the figures grouped around the foot of its staircase, long before he got there.

The younger kids had come straight from Cardiff Road. Jonas was with them, looking cool and in control.

Billy said, "Where's John?"

"Taking the long way round," said Jonas. "Give him a couple of minutes. Any trouble?"

One of the younger kids, who was doubled over, panting, with his hands on his knees, looked up and said, "Yeah, there was trouble. Nearly got caught, didn't I? Some bloke grabbed me."

"Your mate Nick," Billy told Jonas.

"You told us there wouldn't be no trouble," said the kid. "You told us Darker had all that sorted."

"He has," Jonas said.

"Didn't seem like it to me," the kid said with a scowl. "Know what I reckon?"

"What?" said Jonas.

"I reckon you're having us on. I reckon there's no such person as this Darker bloke. You talk about him all the time, but we never see him, do we?

You're making it all up!"

Jonas said, "Am I?" He smiled, slow and dangerous. The blackness of his eye sockets were suddenly lit with a pale glow that gleamed brighter. "Am I?" Jonas said again, in a voice that wasn't his own. "You want the dream again, boy – the one you had last night?" The glow in his eyes was bright enough to cast shadows.

The kid whimpered, made choking noises in the back of his throat; he sank down on to his knees, trembling.

"No!" he whispered. "I didn't mean it, honest!"

"Where am I?" said Jonas.

The kid said, "Everywhere! You're everywhere, Darker!"

10

Carys helped Nick brush dust off his clothes. "What was all that stuff about Darker?" she said.

"It's that name that's been sprayed all over the place," Nick said. "We saw it on one of the stones in Prospect Park at lunchtime."

"Did we?" said Carys. "Can't remember."

Up ahead, Cardiff Road filled with pulsing blue light as a police car pulled up at the kerb.

Carys set her mouth into a determined line. "Come on, Nick," she said. "We're not going to let them get away with this."

The police car was parked next to a short-lease shop that sold imported junk. The front window had been shattered; a few jagged fragments were still in place; pieces of glass were scattered over the pavement, crunching beneath the boots of a policeman who stood with his hands on his hips, surveying the damage. Another policeman was in the car, talking into a handset.

"Excuse me," said Carys.

The policeman outside the shop turned. He had a stubby nose and a ginger-grey moustache.

"We saw the kids who did it," said Carys. "They came running down the street just now."

The policeman didn't move or speak.

"One of them threw a stone at my friend," Carys said.

"Is this your friend?" said the policeman, looking at Nick.

"Yes," said Carys.

"Did the stone hit you?"

"No," Nick said.

"So you're not injured at all?"

"No."

"No harm done then," the policeman said. He seemed strangely unconcerned.

Carys said, "We got a good look at them — especially the one who threw the stone. We could give you a description."

"Very public spirited, I'm sure," said the policeman, "but that won't be necessary."

"But . . . there's been a robbery!" Carys spluttered.

The policeman bared his teeth in what might have been a smile. "Dolls and radio–clocks," he said. "Not exactly top blag, is it? The owner's going to make more out of his insurance than he would have if he'd sold the stuff."

"Aren't you going to take a statement?" said Carys.

"Look," said the policeman, "I could give you the names and addresses of the kids responsible, right now. Most of them are too young to be prosecuted, and the ones who are old enough will have watertight alibis. If I took a statement, it'd take up a lot of your time, and mine, and it'd get us nowhere. You're not hurt, your friend's not hurt, so I suggest you get off home and forget all about it."

It didn't seem real. Nick wouldn't have been surprised to see cameras and lighting-rigs. The policeman was like an actor playing a part. Maybe the shop was a set, made from painted hardboard and filled with props.

"Let's go, Carys," said Nick. "The officer's got work to do."

"That's right!" the policeman said. "You leave it all to us. G'night, now."

Nick took Carys by the arm and led her away.

"I don't believe this!" said Carys. "I do not believe what just happened! He didn't even want to know."

"Leave it," said Nick. "Like he said, we didn't get hurt, so there's no point in getting involved."

"Oh, course not!" Carys said. "Some kids break into a shop, one of them tries to rearrange your face with a rock — happens every day, doesn't it? Nothing to get your knickers in a twist about. And there was I, thinking that it was the police's job to catch criminals."

"The police can't do anything."

"Don't want to do anything is more like! Either the whole town's gone mad, or it's me! Which d'you reckon, Nick?"

Nick wished that he knew.

Carys's bus was waiting at the stop. The doors were closed and the driver was seated at the wheel, reading a newspaper.

Carys said, "Well, it's been an interesting evening."

"Tell me about it!" said Nick.

There was a silence. Nick could feel that he was expected to say something, but he didn't know what it was.

Carys said, "Am I going to see you again?"

"Yes, if you like."

"No," said Carys. "If *you* like."

"How about tomorrow?"

"Can't. Going to Cardiff with Cat, shopping and girlie-talk."

"Thursday, then," said Nick. "Meet me at the book shop, about one."

"You're on."

The driver started the engine and the bus doors hissed open.

Carys went up on her toes and kissed Nick on the cheek. "See you Thursday," she said.

Nick walked home the long way, nervous of what he might meet if he took short-cuts down the dark backstreets. He flashed back over what had happened: the eyes of the boys, the strange behaviour of the policeman.

Maybe it's not just the kids, thought Nick. Maybe something's inside the police too, making them think that it's not worth doing their job properly.

But what could do that?

Anything seemed possible tonight. Something could be lurking in every porch and alleyway he passed, waiting to leap out and attack him.

"Leave it out, Lloyd!" Nick told himself. "Think about something else!"

Like: how much was he going to tell his parents? Better to leave out the bits about the stone-throwing, and the policeman. Mum would go ballistic and make a complaining phone call to the police station. Nick would just say he had seen the gang from a distance.

And Carys – her laugh and overdramatic gestures, the softness of her kiss, the scent of pine in her hair. . .

Nick hung on to anything that would keep him from facing the big question, the one that frightened him so much that it gave him dragging sensations in the pit of his stomach.

Who was Darker?

11

The morning routine of getting up, showered, dressed and having breakfast, made the terrors of the previous night seem trivial – even silly. There was no big mystery. The national newspapers were always running reports about young people turning to crime in areas of high unemployment, and Abernant had more unemployment than most towns in South Wales. The policeman had been tired - how many other break-ins had he been called out to that evening? And Darker had to be some local hard-man, or an adult who organized kids into gangs and then sold what they stole – like Fagin in *Oliver Twist*.

What was it Mr Hicks had said in science? "When faced with a number of different theories to account for a given phenomenon, the simplest theory is the one most likely to be true."

Right! thought Nick. So either some sort of evil force has taken over the local kids and is playing mind-games with the police, or Abernant is experiencing a juvenile crime wave. No contest!

And all the rest, the tension in the air, the look in the boys' eyes, was your imagination. All in your imagination. Nothing to be afraid of.

Nick frowned – whose voice was it that he was remembering? Not Mr Hicks's, or Dad's. It was maddening: Nick knew he had heard the voice before, but he couldn't place it.

Mr Protheroe was in the back room of the shop, reading *Folk Tales & Ballads of Glamorgan*. A cup of cold tea stood near the computer, and Mr Protheroe was so engrossed in the book that he almost leapt out of his chair when Nick came in.

"Sorry!" said Nick. "Didn't mean to startle you."

"Startle me?" said Mr Protheroe. "You nearly sent me to the undiscover'd country from whose bourn no traveller returns."

"*Macbeth?*" said Nick.

"*Hamlet*, untutored churl!" Mr Protheroe looked at the book admiringly. "I must say, old Aspasia Greatorex has a way with words. A little dry in places, but when you get to my age, you acquire a taste for such things. I'm delighted to say he even includes a section on Abernant."

"Really?" said Nick. "But wasn't the book published in 1840 something? I didn't think there was much here before they built the docks."

"Abernant has a far longer history than that," said Mr Protheroe. "It's mentioned in the Domesday book, and there was an excavation in Porthcwm Woods in the 1930s on a site that showed evidence of continuous occupation since Neolithic times."

"I didn't know that," said Nick.

"Of course you didn't. Anything of interest in Abernant gets forgotten as soon as it happens. Like the docks – anywhere else, they would have been turned into a marina and an industrial heritage park – but not Abernant. The burghers of this fair town like to keep themselves to themselves. They don't want a lot of foreign professors poking about, digging up the town's secret past."

"Like the 1890s?" said Nick. "This was a pretty happening spot then, wasn't it?"

"And before," said Mr Protheroe. "Hands clean?"

"Sparkling."

Mr Protheroe offered the book to Nick. "Then you may peruse," he said. "Try the section that starts on page seventeen."

The edges of the book were grey with dust, but

inside the paper was still white. Nick turned to page seventeen and began to read.

The Ballad of Tom Dacre
(As told to the author by Mrs Megan Pritchard of Brynhill Farm, Abernant.)

Tom Dacre was a rascal, a thief and a liar.
He stole bread for his table and kindling for his fire.
He stole butter from the farmer, and the miller's cart,
And a kiss from a maiden, and broke her heart.

So they took Tom Dacre tied in a sack
And carried him far down the forest track
And beat him with cudgels, and left him for dead.
"But that will never stop me," Tom Dacre said.

Then they caught Tom Dacre and bound his arms
And circled him fast with magic charms.
They buried him under earth and stones,
And marked the place with a raven's bones.

But the earth would not hold him, the grave mouth yawned
And Tom sprang into the night, reborn.

"Like a Tom and Jerry cartoon!" said Nick.

"Indeed?" said Mr Protheroe.

"Yes," said Nick. "Tom can get blown up with dynamite, or get a ten tonne weight dropped on him, but he always bounces back. Like the Tom in the poem."

"An astute, if bizarre analogy," said Mr Protheroe. "But read on!"

This ballad, perhaps only a surviving fragment of a longer whole, was taught to Mrs Pritchard by her father, in whose family it had been passed down from generation to generation. Though the ballad is not widely known in Abernant, the name of Tom Dacre is invoked by local matrons as a threat to errant children – in effect, a Welsh "bogeyman". His ghost is rumoured to haunt the woods in the locality. (This may be a folk-memory from the days of the Druids, when such places were venerated as the domiciles of spirits.)

A more intriguing possibility is that Tom Dacre may actually have existed. A fragmentary Assize Roll of 1567 records that a Twm Acre was hung for sheep-stealing. The execution took place at a gibbet erected at a crossroads on the main thoroughfare to Cardiff. This unsavoury event would likely have been the source of great excitement in a rural hamlet, and would doubtless have been recalled in later years, passing inexorably from memory into legend.

Abernant has long been notorious for the disruptive behaviour of its young folk. The Reverend Eli

Watkins (Vicar of St John's Church, Abernant, 1750–1790) wrote an account of an event which occurred on the night of August 3rd, 1783. A group of unruly youths, doubtless under the influence of spirituous liquors, attacked a gypsy pedlar and inflicted such grievous wounds that the poor fellow passed away.

As recently as 1819, a riotous assembly of youths set fire to a local farmer's cow shed. The farmer and one of his sons perished in the attempt to extinguish the blaze. (Though this was told to me by Mrs Pritchard, whose memory is somewhat infirm. I can find no official record of such an event.)

"So young people have been getting out of hand in Abernant for years?" said Nick.

"There's nothing new under the sun," Mr Protheroe said. "The behaviour of Abernant's youth in the past makes fascinating reading, if you can be bothered with all the effort of digging it out. For some reason the town's taken great pains to cover up its history. Take the summer of 1929, for instance."

"What about it?"

"One afternoon, all the local children sat down in the playgrounds of their schools and refused to go to lessons."

A bell rang in Nick's head – where had he seen something about that?

Mr Protheroe's voice dropped to a murmur. "Then, of course, there was 1963—"

"Excuse me a minute," said Nick. "I just want to check something out."

He went into the shop and over to the counter, where *Old Abernant in Photographs* was propped up against the till. Nick riffled through the book, and stopped at a photograph that showed rows of children on banked benches, with the walls and windows of a school in the background. Teachers occupied the front row.

Miserable lot! thought Nick. Not a smile anywhere!

The caption said: *Staff and pupils of Asquith Road School, 1927. Pupils of this school are said to have inspired the so-called School Strike of 1929, which led to the retirement of the Headmaster, Colonel Dafydd Thomas (bottom row, centre).*

Nick looked back at the photograph. Colonel Thomas had a face like a hatchet.

Bet the kids threw a party when he left! Nick thought. Then his chest went tight.

Directly above the colonel was a boy – pudding-basin haircut, baggy shorts, long woollen socks. Even in black and white, the boy's face looked startlingly pale; his eyes were dark, lost, sly.

It was the face of the boy who had thrown the stone at Nick.

12

There was a mini-rush at Bargain Books: an aeroplane-anorak bought *Luftwaffe Camouflage Markings*, and two old ladies hit the *Mills and Boon* shelf.

"That's nine pounds forty closer to my first million!" Mr Protheroe said. "Winter holidays in the West Indies, here I come!"

Nick wasn't listening; he was still trying to explain away the resemblance between the schoolboy in the photograph, and the boy on Cardiff Road. Maybe there was no resemblance, maybe it was just in his imagination; or perhaps the two boys were related, like grandfather and grandson. Faces ran in families, like names. That had to be it, because one thing was certain: little boys didn't stay the same for nearly seventy years; they grew up, got old and died.

Unless. . .

Nick said, "Mr Protheroe, d'you believe in ghosts?"

Mr Protheroe took a sharp breath, as though something had alarmed him; then relaxed and smiled. "You're a bit off the wall today, aren't you?" he said. "What prompted that question?"

"I was just wondering," said Nick. "Aspasia Greatorex mentions a ghost, in his book."

"Oh, I believe in ghosts when I'm reading books!" said Mr Protheroe. "Ever read the stories of M R James?"

"No."

"Take my word for it, when it comes to the ghost story, he's the master!" A far-off look came into Mr Protheroe's eyes. "I must have been twelve when I first discovered him. Got me so worked up, I decided to go ghost-hunting."

"Where?"

"In the cemetery — where else?" Mr Protheroe said. "I climbed over the wall one night and walked around the graves in the moonlight."

"Did you see anything?"

"No. I didn't believe enough."

"I don't follow," said Nick.

Mr Protheroe said, "You know the story about the optimist who says a bottle is half full, and the pessimist who says it's half empty? I think ghosts are like that. You see what you want to see. If you believe in ghosts strongly enough, you'll see them. If you don't, you'll only see yourself."

Nick was confused. "But does that mean ghosts are real, or not?" he said.

"It all depends on what you mean by reality," said Mr Protheroe. "Humanity's been puzzling over that one for centuries. Read some philosophy books if you want to learn about it — but I warn you, philosophers are much better at questions than they are at answers."

"Maybe I should try something less ambitious," Nick said. "Have we got anything in stock about the School Strike?"

"Ah, the fickleness of young minds!" Mr Protheroe said, with a sigh. "They flit from subject to subject like bees in a bed of lavender! You need to consult the *Abernant Centenary Book*. It was published in 1988 to celebrate the town's hundredth birthday. I used to have a couple of copies — unfortunately I sold the last one before you started."

"Any idea of where I could get hold of one?"

Mr Protheroe lifted up his glasses and rubbed the bridge of his nose. "There used to be a place in town called, I believe, the Public Library," he said.

The library occupied part of the ground floor of

the town hall. Nick pushed his way through the revolving door and stood in the foyer, transfixed by the familiarity of the place. Nothing ever changed here – not even the posters on the bulletin board. The same past local dignitaries stared down from the framed photographs on the walls: mayors with moustaches like walrus tusks; plump town clerks with watch-chains stretched across their bulging waistcoats.

To Nick's left was the door to the children's library, the magical place that he had spent years plundering. He remembered how grown-up he had felt when he was first issued with an adult ticket. Then had come the GCSE years, when reading had been about research and coursework. Nick couldn't recall the title of the last book that he had read for fun.

What am I doing here? he thought.

It had seemed a good idea when he left Bargain Books; now he realized that it had been an impulse, and wondered why he had followed it.

The sun is shining outside. Life is going on, and you're missing it. You could be doing something far more interesting than shutting yourself up in a stuffy library.

That strange-familiar voice again. Nick resisted it. Nothing else to do with the afternoon, is there? he thought.

The *Abernant Centenary Book* was on the

reference shelves. Its spine was cracked, and as Nick lifted the book down it sagged, as though the pages were about to open out like a fan.

Falling apart? Well, a book about Abernant would be, wouldn't it?

There was a drawing on the dust cover – an aerial panorama of the town, commissioned by the Docks Company in 1901, according to the caption. In the drawing, the docks were filled with ships, and long coal-trains ran along the railway sidings – a bustling, thriving port.

Nick carried the book to a nearby table, consulted the index and found *School Strike: 285.*

This singular event took place in July 1927, a generation before the term "juvenile delinquency" was coined. . .

Nick groaned inwardly. Nothing worse than a historian who fancies himself as a comedian! he thought.

The account was written as though the whole thing had been a joke, and was pretty tedious going until it came to an interview with a man called William Hart, who had taken part in the strike.

I was a pupil at Dock Road School, and so was my yucker (younger brother) Dan. It was boiling hot that summer, and none of us wanted to be in school. We played a lot of practical jokes on the teachers – and it wasn't just us, it was all the kids in the town. Boys were running round at night, breaking windows and playing Knock-Down Ginger. (Knocking on front doors and running away.)

Anyway, one morning Dan told me about this letter that was supposed to have been written by a boy at Chamberlain Road School. Tommy, or Tony his name was — I don't remember it now. It said that after dinner, all the children in all the schools were going to sit down in the playgrounds and refuse to do as they were told. So we did as well, nearly the whole lot of us.

There was this one teacher, Mr Humphreys — big chap, served in the Machine Gun Corps during the Great War — who tried to get us to go back inside. He tried persuasion, then when that didn't work, he lost his rag. He was waving a cane about, bawling his head off, and his face was as purple as a beetroot. Well, all of a sudden, he had a fit and collapsed. We thought, what with the heat and everything, that he'd fainted. Later, we heard that he'd died of a heart attack.

After Mr Humphreys collapsed, it broke the spell. We all stood up and filed back into school. To this day I couldn't tell you why it happened. It was pure mischief — like an epidemic, sort of thing. Still, kids do get sudden crazes for things, don't they? I remember being mad for collecting cigarette cards. One minute it's all the go, and the next it's something else.

Nick looked up from the book. Aspasia Greatorex had mentioned a pedlar who had been beaten to death in 1783, and a farmer and his son who had died in a fire in 1811. And here's another death in 1927, Nick thought. All connected with the young people of Abernant. Interesting!

He read on; the jokey historian was back.

In many ways, the School Strike has intriguing parallels with the Dock Riot of 1891 (see pages 50–52). Both events may have been in response to a downturn in the economy, but speculation as to the root causes of the School Strike belongs to the realm of the child psychologist, not the historian.

Nick thought, What Dock Riot? How come I've never heard of that, or the School Strike? Grandad must have been in school in 1927, and he's never mentioned them. Funny, you'd think he'd remember something like that.

Nick had always seen Abernant as a quiet, respectable town; it was disturbing to discover that its history had a darker side.

Nick turned to page fifty, only to find that it wasn't there. An entire chapter had been torn out of the book. Who'd do something like that? thought Nick. What's the point?

Somewhere a door opened; a draught blew through the library, flipping over a page of the book.

Nick felt the floor pitch like the deck of a ship at sea.

Words were scrawled on the margin in green crayon: *DARKER IS EVERYWHERE.*

Nick's mind went into overdrive: Darker had known he would find the photograph in Bargain Books, and that he would come to the library to find out more. Darker had torn out the missing chapter, and written in the margin to – what? Tease Nick? Threaten him?

Panic brought Nick to his feet and pushed him out of the library on to Town Hall Square.

There were no ghosts or criminal masterminds, just people walking along, going into and coming out of shops; just Abernant on a summer's afternoon, dilapidated and boring.

I'm cracking up, thought Nick. Post exam-stress trauma. I need to talk to somebody about all this, get it out into the open so I can see for myself how stupid I'm being.

Carys. She would listen; she might even understand what Nick couldn't understand himself. . .

The thudding of an electronic drum broke through Nick's thoughts. A bright yellow convertible was cruising down Cardiff Road, top down, stereo jacked-up full. Louise was in the passenger's seat, eyes hidden behind wraparound shades, blonde hair streaming out behind her, one hand on the driver's shoulder – Geoff Myers's shoulder.

"Oh, great!" Nick whispered. "That's just great!"

13

Nick woke up on Thursday morning thinking of Louise. His memory screened action replays: their first kiss, one cold Sunday morning at the Brynhill shopping precinct; Louise dancing in jittering strobe-lights, every flicker a single frame of film; their reflection in shop windows giving him a glimpse of the couple that others saw. It wasn't just Louise that Nick missed, it was himself — the person he had been when they were together.

The weather matched his mood. A layer of grey cloud covered the sky, turning the sea the colour of cement. It was cooler, but still humid: the recipe for rain. Nick walked along the High Street with something itching in his mind, as if he had forgotten something important; but when he tried to recall what it was, all he could remember was Louise. "Bad day," he thought. "Just get through it and hope that tomorrow will be better."

Strange noises were coming from the back room at Bargain Books – ominous music and cackling laughter.

"Mr Protheroe?" Nick said.

Mr Protheroe was seated at the computer. On the screen, a knight in silver armour was chasing a crone in tattered robes through a murky labyrinth. The crone paused to spit a blue fireball. Mr Protheroe clicked the mouse, and the knight raised his shield.

"What are you doing?" said Nick.

"I'm doing what it looks like I'm doing," said Mr Protheroe. "And if I can just – damn it!"

The knight dissolved into a shower of pixels and the screen filled up with a close-up of the crone's face. Her lips twisted into a mocking smile.

"Loser!" she said.

Mr Protheroe looked at Nick, his expression partly annoyed, partly guilty. "I found out yesterday afternoon that there was a game included in the software bundle that came with the computer," he said. "I thought playing it might improve my mouse skills – and anyway, I needed something to distract my thoughts."

"That right?" said Nick. "I'd be careful if I were you, those games can be addictive."

"And infuriating!" said Mr Protheroe. "I can't get past level one! You, er, couldn't give me a few tips, could you?"

"I haven't seen it before," said Nick. "What's it called?"

"Nightmares in the Witch House."

For a split-second, Nick was somewhere else: he caught a glimpse of long grass in sunshine, but it had gone almost as soon as it was there. "The Witch House?" he said. "Why's that familiar?"

"You're probably thinking of the Witch House in Porthcwm Woods," said Mr Protheroe. "Are they still spinning yarns about it?"

"I think so," said Nick. He was sure that someone had told him the story, a long time ago.

"Like most old tales, there's a grain of truth in it," said Mr Protheroe. "The Witch House was the site I was telling you about, the one that was excavated in the Thirties. They found fragments of glass from an alembic."

"A what?"

"A flask used by alchemists," said Mr Protheroe. "It seems that someone who lived in the house dabbled in the Secret Arts."

"You mean there really *was* a witch?" Nick said.

"Alchemy had nothing to do with witchcraft — more like early experiments in chemistry. Of course, the locals would have thought it was magic. That's what they called everything that they didn't understand. There are things far stranger than witches in Abernant's murky past." Mr Protheroe quit the game and indulged himself in a long stretch. "You know," he said, chewing thoughtfully at the edge of his moustache, "one day somebody will write a book about the *real* history of this town. The only thing is, it would never be published. Who'd believe it?"

Nick spent the next hour pondering Mr Protheroe's words. The real history of Abernant – but what was it? He had tried to find out a little of it in the library, and had been warned off, then distracted.

What if Darker arranged it? Nick thought. Put it into Louise's head to go for a walk with Geoff, then made Geoff drive past the library as I was coming out, so I'd see them and forget about the missing pages in the centenary book... It sounded paranoid. But just because you're paranoid doesn't mean that they aren't out to get you. Nick smiled wryly at himself. OK, go with it. Someone or something, call it Darker, doesn't want anyone who uses Abernant library to find out what happened in 1891. Why not?

At eleven o'clock, Mr Protheroe and Nick had their mid-morning tea.

"Mr Protheroe," said Nick, "where would I find out more about the Dock Riot of 1891?"

Mr Protheroe's eyes went as sharp as a fox's.

"Cardiff," he said. "The Welsh National Industrial and Maritime Museum have got a records office there. I visited it myself last year when I was doing a little research of my own." For a moment, Mr Protheroe's eyes clouded over. "You have to make an appointment in advance. I've got the number in my diary somewhere, if you'd like it. Mr Parry-Edwards is the man you want to talk to."

"Thanks," Nick said.

Mr Protheroe's diary turned out to be a tatty little notebook, stuffed with slips of paper.

"Here we are!" Mr Protheroe said, after a search of several minutes. "I'll write it down for you." He folded up a brown paper bag from the stock under the counter, and scribbled the number down, then paused thoughtfully. "You know, sometimes it's better to leave the past alone, Nick," he said. "If you try to find out too much, you end up knowing more than you bargained for. The past belongs to the people who lived in it – wrinklies, like me."

Nick had the strange feeling that Mr Protheroe was warning him about something, but he couldn't think what.

Carys came into the shop at ten to one. She was wearing a knee-length dress – white with a geometric black pattern – and a black silk baseball jacket. Her smile was dazzling. "Hi!" she said. "Ready to go?"

"In another ten minutes" said Nick.

Mr Protheroe was on the other side of the shop, checking through the books on mythology. "I might just be able to spare you," he said, turning round. "It's not as if—" His eyes widened as he caught sight of Carys. "Land of my fathers, what decade are we in?" he gasped.

Nick and Carys exchanged puzzled looks.

"Forgive my sudden outburst," Mr Protheroe said to Carys. "But you're wearing what, in the Sixties, would have been known as an Op-Art dress."

"Am I?" said Carys, looking down at herself. "I bought it in Cardiff yesterday."

"Fashion!" Mr Protheroe said. "Like the hokey-cokey – in, out, in, out, shake it all about!" His eyes were sad.

Nick said, "If you're sure it's all right, Mr Protheroe. . ."

Mr Protheroe brought his right hand down in a brushing movement. "Off with the pair of you!" he said. "And be sure to dilly and dally – youth's a stuff will not endure!"

Out on the street, Carys said, "Your boss is a bit cuddly, isn't he?"

"You think so?"

"Like a big teddy."

"Sure you don't mean a grizzly?"

Carys tilted back her head and sniffed,

pretending to be offended. "At least he noticed my dress," she said.

"So did I," Nick said defensively. "It looks nice."

"*Nice?*" said Carys.

"I meant, it suits you."

"Better," said Carys, "but a lot of room for improvement. So where d'you fancy going this afternoon?"

"Cardiff," said Nick. "I want to check on something in a museum."

"A museum," Carys, said. "When you get right down to it, you're just a romantic fool aren't you, Nick Lloyd?"

"You don't have to come. It'll probably be boring."

"Not as boring as spending the time on my own," said Carys. "What's it all about, or is that a mystery?

"I don't know what it's about," said Nick. "That's why I have to go to Cardiff, but first I need to make a phone call."

14

Mrs Jones said, "You were late home last night, love."

Jonas swigged the last of his coffee and set the mug down on the kitchen table. "So?" he said.

"I was worried," said Mrs Jones. "Where did you go?"

"Around."

Mrs Jones clenched her fingers anxiously.

"These new friend of yours. . ." she said.

"What about them?"

"I don't know that I approve of them."

"Oh? Which ones?" said Jonas.

Mrs Jones struggled to remember; she was sure that she'd known the names, but somehow they had slipped away from her, lost in the heavy pulse that beat in her temples. "Oh dear," she said. "I think I must be getting a migraine."

Jonas stood up, crossed the kitchen and took his jacket from its peg on the door.

"You going out" said Mrs Jones.

"Yeah."

"What time will you be back?"

"Don't know. Depends."

Mrs Jones had meant to have a good talk with Jonas: he seemed so surly and unhappy these days and she wanted to get to the bottom of it, but when she tried to find the words, the hammering in her head blotted them out.

Jonas left the house and walked through town. He was wearing his headphones, and the volume on the Walkman was turned up to maximum. The wild music was a strange soundtrack to Abernant.

When he reached the docks, Jonas went straight to the railway bridge and mounted the steps. The sky was almost black, and dark veils of rain were edging along the Bristol Channel. The waves in Number One Dock flattened to the shape of the wind.

Are you listening to me, boy?

The voice was louder than the music.

"I'm listening," said Jonas.

We must do something about that friend of yours.

"Who, Nick? Why?"

He's not like the rest. He's an outsider. He thinks he can stand against me.

"No one can stand against you. You're Darker."

He must be taught. You will help me to teach him, you and the others.

"He's harmless," said Jonas. "I just need a bit more time to talk him around, that's all."

Jonas felt Darker's restlessness seethe all around him.

It's too late for that. There is no more time. He must be made to come to us.

"I tried. He didn't want to know."

You must use his weakness.

"Weakness?"

The girl.

"Of course, the girl. I didn't think of that."

Light flickered through the approaching rain. Jonas smiled.

15

The train to Cardiff skirted the edge of the docks' wasteland, then rounded a bend into countryside: farmhouses, small fields stretched together with hedgerows, wooded hills. Nick suddenly felt a pressure release itself inside him, and the surprise of the relief made him laugh out loud.

"Did you feel that?" said Carys.

"Yes."

"Like a rubber band snapping. I noticed it yesterday. When Cat and I got on the train, everybody was quiet, but as soon as we were out of Abernant, they all started talking. Coming back, it was the other way round. Must be something to do with the weather."

Or maybe Darker's affecting the whole town, thought Nick. Everybody's in a trance, and Darker uses them as puppets.

It wasn't a comfortable thought to have, but there was no way for Nick to unthink it.

The records office was on a street that ran from the city centre to the heart of Cardiff's dockland. The building might once have been a shop, but the windows now displayed ships' compasses in brass housings, and casts of Bronze Age axe-heads. In the foyer, time fell apart: a nineteenth-century shipping company's ticket office, with a curved wooden desk and frosted-glass panels, stood next to the bar of a Victorian pub. There were blown-up photographs of collieries and farm-houses; a row of model ships in glass cases.

"Like a big junk shop, isn't it?" said Carys.

"More like a game reserve, with bits of history instead of endangered species," said Nick.

Mr Parry-Edwards was waiting at the reception desk. His smile was friendly and his handshake firm. "I'll show you the way to the reading room," he said. "I've got the documents you wanted. Can't say we get asked for them very often – the Abernant Dock Riot is a bit of an obscure subject. Where did you come across it?"

"In an old book," said Nick. "There wasn't much and I wanted to find out more."

The reading room was small, and most of the space was taken up by a row of tables and chairs. On one of the tables lay a fat book bound in dark-blue leather, with gold lettering on the spine: *Abernant Dock Commissioners' Reports 1880–1900.*

"I've marked the place for you," Mr Parry-Edwards said. His manner became more formal. "Before I let you consult the document, you're required to sign an agreement not to mark or damage it in any way. If you wish to take notes, you must only use a pencil. The consumption of food or drink is not allowed in this room, nor can any document or part of a document be removed from it. If you require any assistance, please enquire at the reception desk." His face softened into a smile. "Sorry about the rigmarole," he said. "Standard procedure. When you've finished, just leave the book on the table, but don't forget to sign out." He glanced at his watch. "And now, if you'll excuse me. . ."

Unlike most of the nineteenth-century prose that Nick had read, the report was written in clear, concise English. It began with a brief description and history of Abernant Docks, then homed in on the night of 17th August, 1891.

At approximately 11 pm, a mob of between thirty and forty youths, some estimated to be as young as seven years of age, ran down Deacon Street in the direction of the docks, breaking windows as they went.

When they reached Dock Terrace, the youths climbed over the iron railing and descended the embankment, on to the railway line. After crossing the line, they advanced towards the coal tips on the northern side of Number One Dock.

Here they were observed by two night-watchmen, Jesse Watts and Walter Ling. Both men left their hut to apprehend the youths, but were met by a hail of coal. Jesse Watts was struck on the forehead and fell stunned to the ground. By the time he had recovered consciousness, the mob had dispersed, but he became aware of splashing and cries for help coming from Number One Dock. He hurried to the dockside, arriving in time to see Walter Ling disappear beneath the surface of the water. Watts dived into the dock in an attempt to rescue Ling, but the water was covered in a thick layer of coal dust which temporarily blinded him, and he was forced to abandon his efforts in order to save himself.

The body of Walter Ling was retrieved from Number One Dock at 8 am the following morning.

At the inquest into Ling's death, held on 8th September, 1891, Sergeant Frederick Buckland of the local constabulary gave evidence that, for some weeks prior to the night of 17th August, the youth of the town had been rowdy and troublesome. Petty larceny, burglary and wanton damage to property had become widespread, despite the police's efforts to contain them. Sergeant Buckland had learned from an informant *that the disruptions had been instigated by an individual called Tam Decker, but a thorough investigation had been unable to reveal the suspect's whereabouts.*

"It's like the other night in Cardiff Road!" said Carys, reading over Nick's shoulder. "The kids run amok while the police stand round like dummies!"

"Tam Decker," Nick said softly. "Tom Dacre."

"Who?"

"A character in an old folk ballad. Someone who keeps coming back from the dead. Dacre. Decker. Darker."

Rain began to fall on the roof of the reading room, and there was a low growl of thunder.

The rain came in sudden bursts, bouncing back off the pavement at waist-height. Gutters choked and flooded, forming miniature lakes. The tyres of passing cars threw out fans of dirty water.

Nick and Carys, caught in the downpour on their way back to the station, ran for the shelter of an arcade and stood panting, shaking raindrops from their clothes.

"D'you think the windswept, natural look will catch on?" Carys said. When Nick didn't respond, she lifted an imaginary telephone receiver to her ear. "Hello, is Nick in, please?"

"Sorry!" said Nick. "Sense of humour bypass."

Carys frowned. "What's the story, Nick?" she

said. "Ever since you read that report in the museum you've been . . . I don't know . . . not with us."

"I've got a lot on my mind."

"Want to tell me about it?"

"I'm not sure I ought to. You'll probably think I'm crazy."

"Try me," said Carys.

Her eyes looked straight into Nick's.

She's the only person I *can* tell, he thought. And if I don't tell someone, I really will flip. He said, "All right, but I warn you, you're going to need that open mind of yours."

Nick began hesitantly, but the need to talk urged him on. He told Carys everything: Darker's name sprayed on the wall of the alley, "The Ballad of Tom Dacre," the torn book in the library, the School Strike and the Dock Riot.

"I thought it was a person at first," he said, "but now I think it's more like a force, an energy that builds up and has to be earthed."

"That's quite a story," said Carys. "Have you been watching a lot of late-night horror movies on TV?"

"I'm serious," said Nick.

Carys said, "I know you are. I was hoping you weren't."

"Just your sort of thing, isn't it? Occult powers, mind control, evil from beyond the grave." Nick tried to laugh but couldn't manage it. "You don't believe me, do you?" he said.

"I'd like to, but. . ." Carys fixed her eyes on the rain falling outside the arcade. "It's Abernant, Nick. Things like that don't happen in Abernant. It's too ordinary."

"I knew you'd think I was crazy."

Carys spoke slowly, choosing her words with care. "You're depressed because of Louise, and you're stressed-out by the exams, and it's made you confused. Yeah, what happened in 1891 is a bit like what's happening now, but it's just a coincidence."

"And the School Strike? And the ballad? And the names? Are they coincidences, too?"

"Your imagination's connecting things that aren't really connected."

"You mean I'm a paranoid schizophrenic," said Nick.

"I don't know what you are," said Carys.

"Neither do I," Nick said. He turned and walked away.

"Nick, where are you going?"

"I need to be on my own for a bit," said Nick. "Give me some space, all right?"

He went out into the rain, with no idea of where he was going.

Carys did not follow him.

Nick didn't notice when the rain stopped. He

trudged the crowded pavements, unaware of anything except his thoughts.

Maybe Carys is right. Maybe I have cracked under the strain – but I *know* all the stuff about Darker sounds mad. Mad people don't think they're mad, do they? According to them, it's everybody else who's peculiar. And if it's just coincidence, then what is it that's coinciding?

It all came back to Darker: Darker could get into people's heads, make them forget things, twist their thoughts like paper clips.

So why not me? How come I can work out what's going on? Why don't I have the Abernant disease?

The answer came like a punch in the face.

Because I'm immune. Something happened to me that inoculated me against it. That's how I can tell what Darker's doing – but why is it doing it?

A desire to know rushed through him, tingling up his backbone. He'd wasted enough time getting carried along by things while he wallowed in feeling sorry for himself – now it was time to do something. He was going to find out what Darker was up to, and try to stop it.

Nick reached Cardiff Central Station in time to catch the 18:15. The carriages were almost full: people piled shopping bags into the luggage racks, chattering to one another about the weather; a few office types hid behind books or newspapers. But as the train approached Abernant, the atmosphere changed, and silence fell like a security grille. People's eyes became glassy, staring at nothing.

Welcome to the Zombie Zone, Nick thought.

His eye was caught by a movement outside. A group of young boys were running alongside the train, dangerously close. One of them raised his arm, and then something smacked against the window next to Nick's face. He ducked, instinctively closing his eyes. When he opened them again, he saw a long crack running from the top to the bottom of the window, looking like a frozen lightning bolt.

None of the other passengers said anything. They sat motionless, their faces blank, as though nothing had happened.

Nick thought, Darker just welcomed me back. It knows that I know.

16

During the night, waves of storms swept over Abernant. The sound of thunder disturbed Nick's sleep, lifting him out of one dream and dropping him into another: he was in year seven, walking into assembly in his pyjamas and slippers; he was in a school production and he hadn't learnt his lines; a long queue of customers was waiting to be served at Bargain Books, and there was no change in the till.

When the alarm clock went off, Nick had to struggle to wake up. Shreds of dreams clung on in his head – or were they memories? The trip to Cardiff, the crack in the train window – had they really happened, or had they been something he had dreamed?

You don't know. You can't tell the difference between what's real and what's not any more.

No.

You can't cope. It's all too much for you, isn't it?

Nick sat up. "Just a minute," he said aloud. "Who the hell am I having this conversation with?"

His mind cleared instantly. This must be how Darker works, he thought. Planting doubts, stirring things up. Well, I'm not giving in. I *was* in Cardiff yesterday, and some kid *did* chuck a stone at the train.

He whispered, "I'm on to you, Darker. This is a fight."

A breeze gusted in through the bedroom window, flapping the curtains.

When Nick arrived at the bookshop, he found Mr Protheroe seated behind the counter, deep in thought, winding his thumbs around each other.

"Morning," Nick said.

"You've got tomorrow off," said Mr Protheroe. "Holiday, with pay."

"How come?"

Mr Protheroe looked up and smiled, but his eyes were evasive. "I have to go to Aberystwyth," he said.

"Didn't that used to be the only town in Wales with more pubs than chapels?" said Nick.

"Perhaps," said Mr Protheroe, "but I'm not

going to sample the delights of the local hostelries. I need to do some research in the archives of the national library."

"Checking up on how much that Aspasia Greatorex book is worth?"

Mr Protheroe shrugged. "Something like that," he said.

"I did some research myself yesterday," said Nick. "I went to the records office in Cardiff that you told me about, to read up on the Dock Riot."

Mr Protheroe narrowed his eyes. "Great minds think alike, fools seldom differ," he muttered; then, in his normal voice, he went on, "You mean to say that you preferred the dusty vaults of academe to the company of your charming young lady?"

"She's not my young lady, she's a friend," said Nick.

Mr Protheroe tutted disapprovingly. "The irony of youth is that by the time you're old enough to appreciate it, it's over!" he said. "The French have a saying – *It's better to waste your youth than to do nothing with it*. Wise words indeed!"

He's in a funny mood, thought Nick. Who's rattled his cage?

"Take the time to live your life, Nick," Mr Protheroe said. "Grab your chances with both hands. You can sort out the world's problems when you're older – and older is something that happens sooner than you might imagine."

Nick said, "Mr Protheroe, what are we talking about?"

"Nothing," said Mr Protheroe. "In all probability, I'm experiencing the early stages of senile dementia. If I had children, I'd bore them with my rambling observations on life, but since I don't, you cop the lot. Just pick out what seems useful and discard the rest."

Nick wondered if Mr Protheroe might be drunk. "Thanks for the advice," he said.

Mr Protheroe's strange mood lasted all morning. Just before one o'clock, he handed Nick an unsealed white envelope. "I won't see you tomorrow, so have your wages now," he said.

Nick did a quick count of the envelope's contents. "You've made a mistake," he said. "There's too much here."

"No mistake," said Mr Protheroe. "I've given you a bonus as a token of my appreciation. Go out for a meal with that friend of yours. Take her on a trip to Cardiff, or Bristol. Get out of Abernant."

Nick smiled ruefully. "Actually, Carys and I had a bit of a falling out yesterday," he said. "I don't think she's talking to me, so I can't see us going anywhere at the moment."

"Then I strongly recommend that you kiss and make up, or whatever the modern equivalent is," said Mr Protheroe. "But make sure that you aren't in Abernant on Saturday night, Nick."

"Why?"

"Because something's going to happen. Something it would be better for you to stay well clear of."

Nick frowned. "What?" he said.

"Don't ask. Just trust me and take my advice. Indulge an old man's whim, will you?"

"I'll do my best," said Nick. He waved the envelope. "Thanks, Mr Protheroe."

"And thank you, Nick," Mr Protheroe said. "Solitary sort of occupation, the second-hand book trade. I've enjoyed your company this summer."

Only later, after he had left Bargain Books, did it strike Nick that Mr Protheroe sounded as though he were saying goodbye.

All the way home, Nick thought about Carys. Can I convince her I'm not a raving loony, or have I blown it completely? Maybe I should ring her up and grovel before she blabs about me to her friends.

But he knew Carys wouldn't do that. He was just making excuses. He wanted to put things right between them because he liked her.

So ring her. Do what Mr Protheroe said, use the extra money to take her out somewhere. If she tells you to get lost, at least you'll know where you stand.

As soon as he got in, Nick looked up Carys's number in the phone book, and called her straight away, so that he wouldn't have a chance to change his mind. When the phone stopped ringing, there was a click, and a man's voice said, "I can't take your call, but if you leave your name and number. . ."

"Damn!" said Nick. He hated using answering machines, but he waited until the beep came and said, "This is Nick Lloyd. I'm a friend of Carys. If she's got time, I'd like her to phone me. I'll be at home this afternoon and this evening." Nick recited his number, remembered to say thank you, hung up, and went into the kitchen to make himself a sandwich. He switched on the radio for background noise, and caught the crashing guitars and whining vocal of the summer's unavoidable hit:

> *You can run but you can't hide,*
> *Cos what I feel won't be denied*
> *And you don't stand a chance,*
> *You just don't stand a chance—*

Nick hit the off button; the song was too much like a message from Darker.

Maybe it's got a job as a DJ, thought Nick. Darker – crazy name, crazy guy! This week's special guest star on *The National Lottery Live*.

It wasn't funny.

Nick took his lunch up to his room and read through the notes he had made while sneaking a look at the Aspasia Greatorex book that morning.

1567 – Twm Acre hung for stealing sheep
1783 – pedlar killed
1819 – farmer and son die in fire

Nick took a biro from the old coffee mug he used as a desk-tidy, and added:

1891 – night-watchman drowned in Dock Riot
1927 – teacher dies of heart attack during School Strike
1999 – ?

Nick was used to dates; he liked them – history was fixed, more certain than the present. He stared at the years, hoping that there was something in them that he could understand and use.

Thirty-six years between 1927 and 1891, he thought. Seventy-two years between 1891 and 1819 – that's twice thirty-six. And then. . .?

He grabbed a calculator.

1819 – 36 = 1783 – 36 = 1747

Nick kept on subtracting thirty-six, until the display said: *1567.*

Darker worked in a thirty-six year cycle – but how far back did it go? Nick remembered the words of Aspasia Greatorex – *Abernant has long been notorious for the disruptive behaviour of its young folk.* How long? What had happened on the dates in the cycle that Nick didn't have any information on?

Not much chance of finding out, Nick thought. Abernant doesn't have much recorded history before the docks were built. But suppose I'm right?

Suppose that every thirty-six years the young people of Abernant go crazy, and someone dies. What does Darker do in between time – sleep?

An uncomfortable picture came into Nick's mind, something he'd seen on a wildlife documentary: an anaconda lying in torpor, its body grotesquely swollen by the slowly-digesting carcass of a wild pig.

Darker comes out to feed! thought Nick. It absorbs all the fear and confusion! They form the energy that keeps it alive! And then people forget what happened, because that's what people in Abernant do – Darker makes them forget.

$1891 + 36 = 1927 + 36 = 1963 + 36 = 1999$

"1963?" said Nick.

Mr Protheroe had said something about 1963. What had happened in Abernant that year – who had died? Nick knew he wouldn't have to go far to find out, because he had his own personal expert on the Sixties: Dad. The obvious thing to do would be to ask him about it – but Dad didn't like talking about his past.

Tricky! thought Nick. Ve-ry tricky!

17

Friday night was Mum's judo night. She left the house at seven, while Nick and Dad were washing up the dinner dishes. When all the plates and pans had been put away, Dad wandered off into the front room, and Nick joined him.

Dad scanned the TV pages of the newspaper. "I don't know!" he grumbled. "Cops and cookery again. I'm surprised they haven't come up with a series about a policeman who's a chef."

"They have," said Nick. "There's cricket on, later."

"Cricket?" said Dad. "I'm not that desperate! Who's beating England this week?"

"The Aussies."

"Cheeky lot! They flog us all their old soaps, then they come over here and—"

The phone rang; Nick sprang from his chair like a startled cat. "I'll get it!" he said as he disappeared into the hall.

"Evidently!" said Dad.

Nick picked up the phone, said, "Hello?"

There was a long silence before Carys said, "Hi, it's me. You asked me to ring."

Nick said, "I'm glad you did. I wasn't sure you'd want to talk to me again after yesterday."

"Did we have a row or something?"

"You could say that, yes."

"I thought we might have, but when I tried to remember it this morning, it was all mixed up."

So Darker got to her, Nick thought. He mentally crossed his fingers and said, "Look, can we meet up somewhere tomorrow? There's a lot I want to tell you, but I can't say it over the phone."

"I thought you worked Saturdays."

"I've got the day off."

Dad came out of the front room and went into the kitchen; Nick heard him filling the kettle.

"I can't make tomorrow morning," said Carys. "Tell you what, I'll meet you at Pebbly Beach, two o'clock, all right?"

"Great. Thanks, Carys!"

As Nick replaced the receiver, he saw that Dad was watching him from the kitchen doorway.

"Girl trouble?" Dad said.

"Kind of."

"I wouldn't be your age again if you paid me," said Dad. "When your hormones kick in, your brains go out the door. I made a lot of mistakes before I found your mum. I still don't know why she married me, but God knows where I'd be if she hadn't. Inside a bottle, probably. That's where I was when we met — well on the way to becoming an alkie."

"Was that because of Julie?" said Nick.

Dad looked surprised. "Your mum told you about her?" he said.

"Just that you'd been married before, that's all."

The kettle came to the boil and switched itself off; Dad didn't notice, his eyes were seeing another time. "We were just kids really, only a couple of years older than you," he said. "My parents tried to warn me, but . . . teen rebel, wasn't I? We started our first row on the way out of the registry office and it didn't stop until five years later, when Julie took off with this bloke from London. Never did anything by halves, did Julie. Went for everything full on."

Nick took a deep breath and said, "Tell me about 1963, Dad."

Dad's eyes came into sharp focus. "What?" he said.

"Something happened in Abernant in 1963, didn't it?"

Dad smiled wryly. "Funny old world!" he said. "Why?"

"Because I haven't thought about it for years — like I'd completely forgotten. But just the last two or three weeks, I've been dreaming about it. What d'you want to know for?"

"Someone mentioned something that got me interested," said Nick. "Anyway, all that Sixties and Seventies stuff is coming back."

"I hope not," said Dad. "Perish the thought!"

Dad sat on the front room sofa, nursing a mug of tea, taking swigs from it as he told his story. His head was framed by the bay window with its view of the street outside; above the rooftops, the sky was yellow with sunset.

Dad said, "Back then, if you were a teenager in Abernant, you had to belong to a tribe. There were still some Teds around, left over from the Fifties — all quiffs and crêpe-soled shoes — but they didn't count. They were blokes in their twenties, old men as far as people my age were concerned. You could be a Rocker, which meant jeans, leather jackets, motorbikes and rock'n'roll, or a Mod — suits, parkas, short hair, scooters and Ska, a sort of early Reggae. In places like London, Mods popped pills called purple hearts — speed — but in Abernant the preferred recreational drug was booze."

"Were you a Mod or a Rocker?" said Nick.

"Bit of a Rocker, I suppose," said Dad. "I loved motorbikes. I used to go to the speedway track in Cardiff, not for the races, but for the machines. Just listening to them rev up made me come over all unnecessary. My only ambitions in life were to get laid and own a motorbike, and I didn't care which order they came in.

"Right from the off there was aggro between Mods and Rockers – bit of name-calling, the occasional punch-up – but in the summer of sixty-three it got really bad. As soon as the schools broke up, there was this . . ." Dad searched for the right word, ". . . atmosphere, you know? A buzz on the streets.

"Mod or Rocker, *the* place to go was Dalmore Bay. You hung out in coffee bars, or stood round the haunted house on the fairground, because it had this gadget that blew girls' skirts up when they stepped on it. And then, at some point, there'd be a bundle."

"What's that?"

"It started off like a playground game," said Dad. "You'd get a gang of Mods and a gang of Rockers at opposite ends of the esplanade, and they'd charge each other, pushing and shoving. Of course, one day someone threw a lucky punch and decked some kid, and then it was – *they got one of ours today, we'll get two of theirs tomorrow* – and it went on from there. Some of the older kids started packing knives and chains, not to use, mind, just to look tough. And all the Rockers were talking about this guy, T D."

Tom Dacre, thought Nick. He felt as if an ice-cube had melted on the back of his neck. "T D?" he said.

"Yeah," said Dad. "No name, just the initials T D. That was the height of cool then. T D was cracked up to be the Rocker's Rocker. Rode a big, blood-red Harley-Davidson, specially tuned, dressed in black leathers and always wore shades, even at night. Some reckoned he was from the Valleys, others said he was from Tiger Bay, but everybody said that T D was a real hard man. He was going to come to Abernant some night, and sort the Mods out good and proper."

"Did you meet him?" Nick said.

"No one did," said Dad. "Kids said they knew someone who knew T D but nobody had actually seen him themselves. Maybe he didn't exist. Maybe he was one of those stories people spread around – like that woman who's supposed to have bathed her dog and put it in the microwave to dry."

"An urban myth," said Nick.

"Myth or not, T D was real that summer," Dad said. "We all believed in him, even the Mods, except that according to them, T D was a Mod from London. Led a gang who rode black scooters, and the gang was going to come down from

London to give the Rockers a seeing-to. I suppose if we'd stopped to think, we would have seen how crazy it was – but nobody was doing much thinking. We were more interested in sinking flagons of cider and duffing one another up."

Lies, rumours and chaos, thought Nick. Sounds like Darker's style.

"Anyway," said Dad, "this Saturday night came, and it was *the* night. T D was definitely going to put in an appearance, and there'd be a bundle to end all bundles. Must have been about two hundred kids on the esplanade, and you could smell trouble a mile off."

"Didn't the police do anything?"

"Too scared," said Dad. "A squad car cruised by once, but it didn't stop. All the kids cheered because it was *our* night – up yours to the police and the older generation.

"It had rained that afternoon, and the roads were slippery. I remember the neon signs on the arcades shining on the pavement. A lot of kids were getting tanked up, but nobody needed booze, we were on an adrenalin-high.

"Half-ten came and went, no T D. The kids were really edgy by then. Someone lobbed a bottle, and when it broke, that was it – geronimo! There were fists flying everywhere, kids lying on the ground having the boot put into them . . . I couldn't take it. I don't know if I had an attack of common sense or just chickened out, but I had to get away. I legged it off the esplanade, up Bay Drive. It was like I'd been dreaming, and I woke up, and the nightmare was still going on. I didn't stop until I ran out of breath at the bottom of Station Hill. This Mod went past on a scooter, and then two Rockers, bikes on full throttle, chasing him. I saw the tail lights go over the top of the hill, and then. . ." Dad paused. "I didn't see the next part – I must have heard about it – but the Mod on the scooter went tearing up Cardiff Road, and just before he came to the town hall, he lost it. The scooter went into a skid, mounted the kerb and hit a young couple passing by. The girl was knocked through a plate–glass window, killed straight out. Only eighteen. Heather something her name was – or was it Hazel?

"After that night, it all went quiet. Nobody talked about the bundle, like we were all ashamed. I couldn't understand how so many people could have been so stupid at the same time. I stayed in for a week, too frightened to put my nose outside the door . . . then I forgot about it. It's like that when you're young, you get over things quickly. Four years later it was the Summer of Love. Kids who'd knocked seven bells out of one another in sixty-three were hugging, passing flowers around. Strange. . ."

"What happened to the Mod on the scooter?" said Nick.

"No idea. Probably got done for driving without due care and attention. I can't remember reading about it. Maybe the police got on to the local papers to hush it up, because the whole business made them look so pathetic. That's typical of Abernant, isn't it? Least said, soonest mended."

Behind Dad's head, the window was filled with shadow, and the streetlights blinked on.

Nothing mended, thought Nick. Darker pigged out on all the negative emotions and disappeared to sleep it off. But it's back now, and it's hungry.

Dad said, "So now you know, and that's enough strolling down memory lane for one night."

"How come you don't like talking about the past, Dad?" said Nick.

"When you've got a past like mine, it's best forgotten. Besides, I promised myself I'd never be one of those nostalgic types. You can't relive the past, and the future hasn't happened yet. That's why you've got to make the most of now — it's all there is." Dad laughed at himself. "Get me!" he said. "I sound like someone on Thought for the Day."

Mum got in just after nine. Her face was drained and her hands were shaking.

"What's up?" said Dad.

Mum said, "I was driving up Cardiff Road just now, and this car pulled out of Deacon Street right in front of me. I had to stand on the brakes! It went up Victoria Street like a bat out of hell. And it was kids — young teenagers! They couldn't have been old enough to drive."

"Joy riders," Dad said grimly.

"I didn't get much joy out of it!" said Mum. "They took ten years off my life! What are the parents thinking of, letting kids that age run round the streets at night?"

"Who knows?" said Dad. "All down the pub, I expect."

"And where were the police?" Mum said.

"Overworked and underpaid, like the rest of us."

"Well, I'm sorry, but that's just not good enough!" said Mum. "Something's got to be done, or someone's going to get killed!"

It was too hot to sleep under the duvet. Nick lay on top of the bed, staring into the dark, thinking. Mum's right, someone *is* going to get killed, just like all the other times. Things will get worse and worse, and then someone will die. Darker will get its fix, and vanish until 2035!

Would it be an accident, like 1963? *Had* it been an accident, or did Darker select its victims, maybe give them a glimpse of what was going to happen so that it could enjoy their fear?

Who will it pick this year? Nick thought.

18

They came at sundown in the gathering shadows, trailing along the road that ran through the docks. The older boys led the way; the younger ones straggled behind, stopping to light the cigarettes that they hoped made them look tough, shoving each other and joking.

The joking stopped when they reached the railway bridge and saw Jonas coming down the steps towards them. The witch-light shimmered in his eyes, and it held them so that no one could look away.

Jonas said, "Up to now it's been kids' stuff, spraying walls and winding up old ladies, but tomorrow night will be different. Tomorrow night is ours, and no one can take it away from us, not parents, not the police, nobody."

"What are we going to do?" someone asked.

"Darker will tell you," said Jonas. "You'll dream about it tonight – the time, the place, everything. And when tomorrow night comes, you'll *be* there. We're in it together, and Darker will deal with anyone who tries to back out."

Each boy had a different thought about what Darker might do, and they all shuddered.

"We belong to him now," Jonas said. "We have to do what he tells us."

He turned to one of the younger boys. "I want you to take a message to a friend of mine tomorrow afternoon," he said.

"What message?" said the boy.

Jonas's eyes widened. The light in them went into the boy's eyes and stayed there, gleaming faintly. The boy's lips writhed and his teeth chattered together; then he said, "Yes. Yes, I'll tell him. Yes, I understand." Talking to the voice in his head that only he could hear.

19

At breakfast, Mum said, "Doing anything special with your day off?"

Nick swallowed a mouthful of toast. "I'm meeting Carys this afternoon," he said. "We might go somewhere – all depends on what she wants to do."

Mum said, half-teasing, half-curious, "Getting serious, is it?"

"Not the way you mean," said Nick.

Dad looked at Nick over the top of the newspaper. "Well, I hope she doesn't jerk you round like the last one did. Proper little Hitler, she was," he said, then grunted as Mum kicked him under the table for being insensitive.

A few days ago, Nick would have been offended

by Dad's remark; now he saw that there was a lot of truth in it. Louise *had* jerked him around: always late for dates, playing little power games to test her hold over him. He had spent the last month remembering her in a rosy, regretful glow, forgetting how inconsiderate and selfish she had been at times.

Dad said, "If you're at a loose end this morning, you can always come to Tesco's with us. We'll walk around smiling, like a family in an advert."

"All right," said Nick.

Dad looked shocked. "I was only joking!" he said.

"I'm not," said Nick. "I've got a lot on my mind, and Tesco's would the perfect place not to think about it."

"I don't know what's wrong with you, but don't give it to me, right?" said Dad. "If Tesco's is the cure, I definitely don't want the illness!"

On the drive to the supermarket, Nick noticed a group of kids clumped together at a bus stop. They looked moody and agitated, like football fans whose team had just lost an important match.

Mum said, "I wonder if any of that lot were in the car I saw last night?"

"Leave it," said Dad. "And if you do see them anywhere, don't try anything stupid, like a citizen's arrest!"

"Least said, soonest mended?" said Nick.

"No," said Dad, "but I don't fancy having the car trashed, or getting a brick through the front room window."

"So I should be like everybody else in Abernant, should I?" said Mum. "Complain, but don't do anything. Let the kids run riot – who cares?"

"I do," said Dad. "But going after them alone isn't going to help. You'll turn yourself into a target. Things will settle down after school starts in September."

"Of course they will!" Mum said sarcastically. "Be the teachers' problem then, won't it? They can take the blame for all the trouble. I'm sick of doing nothing! I'm going to call a meeting of the Neighbourhood Watch and get some night patrols organized."

"It'll make things worse!" Dad warned.

"Dad's right, Mum," said Nick. "When word gets out, the kids will deliberately pick on our street to show how big they are."

Mum said, "Humph!" – which meant that she could see Nick's point, but wasn't willing to say so.

The supermarket was busy. Piped music came out of the loudspeakers in the ceiling, bland as a Eurovision entry. The music was intended to keep people on the move, and soothe them into a mild hypnotic trance – but this morning it didn't seem to be working. Tempers were frayed; people exchanged dirty looks when their trolleys gridlocked, and parents were sharp with their whining offspring.

Nick went supermarket-blank, let the mindless routine cosy him, while he asked himself the questions he always asked, like, Does the world really need tins of Barbie-shaped pasta? and, What are baby vegetables about?

It happened when he was least expecting it. There was a sudden crash, a cry of alarm and outrage. Nick turned, and saw two boys on line-skates zipping up the aisle, weaving round the customers in their way, faces dark with glee.

Behind them, a voice shouted, "Bloody little idiots!"

The boys came close enough for Nick to feel the breeze in their wake; they swerved left at the top of the aisle and glided out through the exit's automatic doors.

At the far end of the aisle, a group of concerned-looking people had gathered around a middle-aged woman whose shopping basket had been knocked out of her hands. A broken bottle of tomato ketchup lay on the floor in a ragged red star.

Mum made a move towards the exit; Dad caught her by the arm. "Take it easy!" he said. "They'll be long gone by now."

Mum said, "But—"

"Let's finish the shopping," said Dad. "You can sort out the world's problems later."

It reminded Nick of what Mr Protheroe had said the previous morning. But suppose you leave it until it's too late to sort anything out? he thought. What happens then?

Carys was late. Nick sat on the promenade wall, the merciless sunshine making him feel increasingly like a sausage on a barbecue. At a quarter to three he gave in, and bought two cartons of chilled fruit juice from the ice-cream van at the edge of the promenade car park. He chugged down the first one, then paused, knowing that if he drank the second one straight away, it would make him feel sick.

Come on, Carys! Nick thought. He took a phonecard from his pocket and turned it over in his fingers. There's a call box on Lake Road. Should I ring her?

But Carys might turn up after he had gone, and assume that he had stood her up. Nick couldn't afford to let that happen – she might never speak to him again.

But what if something's wrong? A car accident, or—

A shadow fell across Nick's face. He looked up, and everything went still and quiet.

The young boy was grinning at him. He had

mousy hair, so short that his scalp showed, and there were silvery patches of flaking skin on his face. "Change of plan," he said.

"What?" said Nick.

"Got a message for you," the boy said.

"Oh, who from?"

The boy said nothing, but drew his grin tighter.

"What d'you want?" said Nick.

"Your little friend's not coming," the boy said.

"*What?*"

"The girl's not going to turn up."

"How d'you know?" said Nick. "What's going on?"

"She's all right, but if you want her to stay that way, you'd better find her."

This can't be real! thought Nick. It isn't happening! He slowly closed his eyes, and opened them. The boy was still there. Nick said, "Are you telling me Carys has been kidnapped?"

"I'm just telling you what I was told to tell you."

"And who told you?"

"I heard it around, you know?" said the boy. "Like, all around."

Nick said, "Darker sent you , didn't he?"

The boy rolled his eyes, "Whoo, scary!" he said. "You don't mess with Darker. If you do, you get your brains scrambled. When Darker says jump, you jump!"

"Suppose I go to the police?"

The boy laughed, folding over like a half-closed book.

If I go to the police, they won't do anything, Nick thought. I'd just be wasting my time.

"That's right," the boy said. "You have to find her yourself, or. . ."

Or what?

The boy shrugged.

And Nick *knew*. It was Carys. She was the one that Darker had chosen to be its victim. "Where is she?" he said.

The boy's face was as grey as a dead light-bulb. His voice changed, became deep and gravelly.

"She's where your fear is, boy!" he said.

"What does that mean?"

The boy began to sing in a tuneless croak, "And you don't stand a chance, you just don't stand a chance." He was a shell with something inside; any second now it would crawl out of him and show itself.

Revulsion made Nick edge away; then he stood and ran. He didn't know where he was going and it didn't matter – as long as he put as much distance as possible between himself and whatever was using the boy to talk.

20

When Nick's panic left him, he found that he was in Meadow Park. He sat on a bench next to a tiered rock garden. Water tumbled over the tiers, down to a small pool. In the pool, fat orange goldfish swam lazily. They were calming to watch, and Nick's mind began to work methodically. He had to find Carys, but where should he start looking?

She's where your fear is, boy.

A riddle. It had been riddles all along – the Aspasia Greatorex book, finding out about the School Strike, the Dock Riot, the thirty-six year cycle – each one leading on to the next like the ascending levels of a computer game.

Who wrote the program? thought Nick. Darker?

It's there, with Carys, and it wants me to work out where that is.

It had to be a place; somewhere he had been badly frightened. Nick ran through the possibilities: his bedroom at night when he was a child; the dentist's surgery; the Headmaster's office; the school hall, lined with rows of exam desks. . . "And Porthcwm Woods," he said quietly.

Every time he thought of Porthcwm Woods, he remembered a flash of something – this time he forced himself to hang on to it.

A picture, his eyes were the camera: trees and tall grass, a peculiar scent. The light in the picture faded, but the scent stayed. Nick breathed it in deeply, and remembered. . .

Nick ran between the trees, sunshine and shadows flicking across his face. In places, banks of stinging nettles leaned over the path, and he struck them aside with the long stick in his right hand. That morning he had watched an episode of *The Quest of the Black Knight* on children's TV, and in his imagination he was the Black Knight, riding his faithful steed Ebony, cutting down enemies with his sword. Nick could hear Jonas and Dando behind him, whooping and laughing as they tried to catch him up, but he knew they wouldn't; he had always been the quickest of the three.

The path forked up ahead and Nick veered to the

left, past a scrub oak with a clump of brambles at its foot. Nick ran into a clearing, and then halfway across it he stopped so suddenly that his teeth clicked together.

On the far side of the clearing was a rose bush, overgrown and leggy, its branches sagging under the weight of the windblown flowers. In front of the bush were the remains of a wall, a ragged line of limestone chunks almost hidden by the long grass. The breeze shifted, carrying a sweet, rotten scent, like handcream and old grass-cuttings.

Nick stood still, feeling sweat trickling through his hair and down the back of his neck. The clearing was as quiet as the inside of a church: no birds sang, no insects hummed through the sunlight. It was a secret place, a place Nick knew he shouldn't be, as certainly as if there had been a *Trespassers will be prosecuted* sign.

What do you want, boy?

Nick started and wheeled around. No one; nothing. The seed-heads of the grass seemed to be rocking with scornful laughter. The voice must have been in his mind.

Another voice came, from Nick's memory this time – Dad's voice, saying something so familiar that Nick whispered along with it. "An over-active imagination, that's what you've got, Nicholas." Dad had said it hundreds of times when Nick was younger, through years of nightmares and the monsters that lived in his bedroom when the lights went out. In the end, Nick had used his imagination against itself, picturing a glass dome over his bed, a dome studded with revolving machine guns that pumped out streams of silver bullets to protect him from the vampires and werewolves that stalked his dreams. . .

Jonas and Dando blundered into the clearing. Dando, face flushed red, bent over and pressed his hands against his chubby knees, puffing as though he were blowing out the candles on a birthday cake one by one. Jonas looked around, his shock of hair shining like a halo. He rolled his eyes and used his creepy voice to say, "This is the Witch House!"

"What Witch House?" Dando panted.

"Don't you know about the Witch of Porthcwm Woods?" said Jonas.

"No."

"Me, neither," said Nick. "I don't know which witch is which!"

Jonas groaned at the old joke, then started pacing about, waving his hands through the air in the same way as when he had been King Herod in the Christmas play. "Long, long ago, there was a cottage here," he said. "An old woman lived in it, all alone. And over that way", he pointed to his right, "was a big farm. Well, one day the farmer noticed that his cows kept getting thinner and thinner, and he couldn't understand it, so he sent for the vet."

"Did they have vets back in them days?" said Dando.

Jonas ignored the interruption. "The vet looked at the cows, but there was nothing wrong with them, except that they had these funny bite-marks on their necks, and he couldn't tell what had caused them.

"So one night, the farmer stayed up to watch over the herd, and just after midnight he saw a ginormous bat – about this big" – Jonas stretched his arms wide – "come flapping out of Porthcwm Woods. It landed on the neck of one of the cows and started sucking its blood. The farmer shouted, and the bat flew up, and the farmer shot at it – POW! He hit it in the wing, but the bat kept on going and the farmer followed it here. He saw it fly through the window of the old woman's cottage. The farmer knocked and knocked at the door, and when the old woman opened it . . . he saw that her left arm was bleeding."

Nick felt the air go cool as midnight. He could see the old woman's face, shrunken and shrivelled, and the gleam of blood in the light of a tallow-lamp.

"And?" said Dando.

"And what?" Jonas said.

"What happened next?"

"Well, I don't know, do I?" said Jonas. "My nan told me the story, and that's all there was. There's another story about the woods, though. See, there was this—"

"I've heard enough of your nan's stupid stories!" Dando grumbled. "Let's go back over Pebbly Beach and look for crabs in the rock pools."

"No!" said Jonas. "Let's find a load of flat pebbles and have a skimming contest. Bet I can skim a stone further than you can."

"Bet you can't!" said Dando.

They wandered off, so caught up in their argument that they failed to notice that Nick was not following them. He felt that something awful would happen if he took a step. The shadow under the trees beyond the clearing twitched, weaving itself into shapes.

A voice came in the sighing leaves and rustling grass: *You can hear me, can't you, boy?*

"Yes."

You woke me up, and it's not time. I'm not ready to wake yet. Go away!

The voice was all round Nick, as though the woods were talking to him.

Don't come back here, boy! Forget that this happened! It's only your imagination. A daydream, that's all it is.

"A daydream," Nick repeated.

There's nothing to be afraid of here.

But there *was* something to be afraid of: Nick could see it gathering in the darkness, focusing like a beam of black light.

Nick dropped his stick and ran. He didn't know

what was happening in the clearing, only that he had to get away from it. His breath shrieked in his throat, and the pounding of his feet on the ground matched the thumping of his heart. He didn't stop running until he collided with Jonas and Dando and the three of them went sprawling.

A nettle lashed Nick's cheek with its hot sting.

"Look where you're going, will you?" said Jonas.

"I think I just killed my leg!" Dando groaned.

Nick sat up, frowning. When he tried to remember why he had been running, his mind went hazy.

"What's the matter with you?" said Jonas. "Seen a ghost, or something?"

"I didn't see anything," said Nick. "I was afraid that. . ."

"What?"

"That you'd leave me behind," Nick said.

Dando stood, and gingerly tried his weight on his right foot. "You're weird, Nick Lloyd!" he said.

"Nuttier than a box of Snickers," Jonas muttered.

"Nuttier than a lump of squirrel-poo!" said Nick.

And they all laughed. . .

You woke me up, and it's not time.

It was the voice of the presence he'd felt at the crazy-golf course, and on the night Mr Thomas's car had been damaged. He had been feeling it all summer, without realizing.

That's where I met Darker before! Nick thought. That's what made me immune. The Witch House is its hiding place. That's where Carys is!

He would have to ring Mum and Dad to let them know that he wouldn't be in for dinner, then—

"Don't think – just do it!" Nick said to himself. He kept repeating the words as he got off the bench and left the park.

21

Nick stood on the crest of Porthcwm Hill and looked down into the valley. He could see a deserted car park and beyond it, the arches of the railway viaduct. They were interruptions, temporary things; the valley really belonged to the trees, and the evening shadows that were rising like a tide. Farms had come and gone, the docks had been built and closed down, Abernant had grown from a village to a town, but the wildness of the valley had remained untouched.

Nick walked towards the wildness.

At the foot of Porthcwm Hill was a stream, crossed by a hump-backed bridge. Nick stopped on the bridge to get his bearings. It wasn't easy to remember after eight years, and the longer he stood still, the more uneasy he became. Porthcwm Woods was a popular local beauty spot, but not many cared to visit it after sundown; Nick could understand why.

The Witch House must be further down, he thought, because we went straight from there to Pebbly Beach.

He followed the road, aware of the sounds around him: the combined evening songs of the birds made a noise like an audience in a theatre before the house lights dimmed. The first pale stars were out, and a blue-grey moon, three-quarters full.

Nick's stomach complained of lack of food. Mum and Dad will be phoning the Indian take-away now, he thought. Or maybe Dad's knocking together one of his special pizzas. . .

He stopped, went back two steps and turned his head from side to side. There was a pocket of silence among the trees; no birds singing. Strange, Nick thought. He left the road, walked towards the silent place and saw a path, heavily overgrown with nettles and thistles. The trees on either side of the path formed a black throat with their branches. Nick let the throat swallow him.

Fear came, like a steel band tightening around his chest. Nick swallowed a coppery taste on the back of his tongue. The thorns of a bramble plucked at the leg of his jeans like fingers trying to restrain him. He reached a fork in the path that he remembered from nightmares, turned left, and walked into the clearing.

The same wall, rose bush, tall grass; the same darkness under the trees – nothing had changed. It was as if the place had been preserved just as Nick had left it, so that Darker could keep the memory of the boy who had accidentally woken it.

Is this all? thought Nick. I've been having nightmares about this place all my life, and it's nothing! It's just ordinary.

"Nick."

The voice made him start. He crouched, his eyes scanning the shadows.

A shape moved among the trees at the far side of the clearing and stepped into the open.

"Carys!" said Nick. "Are you OK?" He took two paces towards her, then faltered to a stop. "Carys?" he said.

There was no recognition in Carys's eyes. She stood with her arms at her sides, her face as lifeless as a dummy's.

Nick swallowed a groan. "What's Darker done to you, Carys?" he said softly. He looked angrily round the clearing. "What's this, Darker?" he said. "A demonstration of what you can do, so I'll be frightened? Hoping to put me off? Come on, show yourself. I know you're here somewhere!"

Another shape stepped out of the trees.

Nick laughed in surprise. "Jonas?" he said. "What the hell are you doing in—" His voice went to nothing as he saw that Jonas wore the same dead expression as Carys.

"We've been waiting for you, Nick," Jonas said. "Darker knew that if the girl came here you'd come looking for her, and you did. Darker's always right."

A lot of things that had been bothering Nick about Jonas began to make sense.

"When did Darker first get to you, Jonas?" said Nick. "During the exams, or before that? That's why you've been so weird this summer. It *was* you I saw in the street the other night, wasn't it?"

"You don't understand what it's like, Nick," said Jonas. "When Darker takes over, you can do anything. Nothing matters except Darker. You're unlocked, you know? Free."

"You're not free!" Nick snorted. "Darker's using you, can't you see that? It has to be stopped, or somebody's going to get killed."

Jonas smiled. "And you think you're strong enough to stop Darker, do you? You have to be taught."

"Taught what? What are you talking about?"

"This," said Jonas. His head jerked back and his body went into spasm, arms windmilling. A light sprang into his eyes, filling the sockets until they were a blank glow.

It wasn't Jonas any more. Something had entered

him, something that moved his lips and said, *You're strong, aren't you, boy? I knew you would be, from the first moment.*

"Darker," said Nick.

If you like. One name's as good as another.

"I'm not letting you in my head. I'm taking Carys out of this!" said Nick, moving forwards.

The light in Jonas's eyes flashed, and Carys screamed.

Be still, boy! I may not control you, but I control her. I can make her feel pain if I wish.

Nick stood still. "Leave her alone!" he said.

Did you really think it would be that easy — that you could simply come here and take the girl away with you? You disappoint me. I thought that you understood me better than that.

"What d'you want me to do?" said Nick.

Amuse me! Shall I make you choose between your life and hers? Shall I make you beg?

Nick said, "You can't make me do anything I don't want to do! You can't harm me, because you can't get inside me. That's your weakness, isn't it? You can't do anything yourself, you have to use people to do things for you, like you're using Jonas."

True, but you underestimate me. You seem to forget that there are those who lack your strength of will.

Nick heard the sound of a car engine, and turned to look. The beams from a pair of headlamps were sweeping down Porthcwm Hill. In a wild moment of hope, Nick thought that someone must have alerted the police, and that a patrol car had been sent to investigate – but then he remembered: the police were powerless. Darker had drained their will in the same way that he had drained Jonas and Carys of theirs.

A twig snapped; Nick levelled his eyes. A teenage boy stepped into the clearing, and another, and another; younger boys stepped out to join them, surrounding Nick in a circle. The boys' faces were expressionless. They stood, staring with sightless eyes, silent in the glow of the brightening moon. They held pebbles; thick sticks.

You see how it is, don't you, boy?

And Nick *did* see. It was a trap: Darker had used Carys as bait to bring him to Porthcwm Woods.

He was the one Darker had chosen.

Nick glanced around, wondering where the first blow would come from. "Listen, Jonas, you can stop this!" he said. "You don't have to do what Darker tells you! None of you does! Darker's in your mind, making you think things that aren't true. If you fight against it, you can—"

You're wasting your breath. They can't hear you. They don't even know where they are, and they won't until this is over. Then they'll forget what happened, because it will be too frightening for them to remember. Are you ready to beg yet, boy?

Something struck Nick's left elbow, and a pebble thudded to the ground. The pain shot up Nick's arm in a sickening jolt of cold pins and needles. Nick cried out as a red mist came down in front of his eyes.

That's right, boy, scream. You'll long for death before I've done with you.

Nick clutched his numb arm and looked wildly round, wondering where the next blow would come from. Would they strike one at a time to prolong the agony for Darker's enjoyment, or rush at him in a frenzy? He lost his footing, stumbled sideways and heard someone crashing through undergrowth. A voice shouted, "Nick? Are you there?"

A bulky, bearded figure was hurrying down the path towards the clearing.

Nick's voice cracked in a sob as he said, "Mr Protheroe?"

22

Mr Protheroe placed his hands on the shoulders of the two boys blocking his way and pushed them aside. They made no attempt to stop him – Mr Protheroe might have been shifting pieces of furniture. He stepped between them, crossed the clearing and stood beside Nick.

It wasn't the Mr Protheroe that Nick knew: his face was harder, craggier and his eyes burned fiercely.

Mr Protheroe stared at Jonas. "Let the children go!" he said loudly. "This is between you and me!"

Darker's cruel laughter filled Nick's head.

You? I broke you long ago.

"Almost," said Mr Protheroe. "But you left me my sorrow, and that was a mistake. It kept my memory alive, made me want to know. I've been waiting for you."

And now I'm here, what do you intend to do?

"To end it," said Mr Protheroe. "I'm going to send you back."

Darker laughed again, and the sound was huge.

Back? You understand nothing, little man. You're too civilized, your mind is too small.

Mr Protheroe began to speak in a language that Nick didn't recognize; his voice rose and fell in a rhythmic chant.

All around the clearing the trees were moving, thrashing their branches, bending their tops as though they were caught in a gale. Leaves sailed into the sky, forming a cloud that wavered like a flock of roosting starlings.

Mr Protheroe didn't flinch; the chant rolled on relentlessly.

Something moved in the grass at Nick's feet: a trickle of blackness, a shadow-snake slithering along; the floor of the clearing was alive with them.

Mr Protheroe was sweating freely and there were lines of strain around his mouth. The effort of keeping up the chant was draining him, and he seemed to be crumpling like a paper bag.

A bough groaned, split with a crack and crashed to the ground. The clearing became still.

Jonas's jaws opened wider than seemed possible, and light streamed out of his gaping mouth. The light was an intense green-white, like the flame of burning magnesium. Mr Protheroe put an arm up to shield his eyes. He was breathing heavily, but the chant did not falter.

Nick narrowed his eyes to slits, and saw the light coming from Jonas form itself into a globe that drifted into the air like a soap bubble. Inside the globe, something twitched. Nick thought he made out a head, a face that wasn't human, limbs drawn up to make a shape like an embryo in the womb.

The globe quivered, and hurtled into the sky, accelerating as it went, dwindling to a dot no bigger than a star; then smaller; then nothing.

Mr Protheroe said, "*In Memoriam, Helen Lewis. Requiescat in pace.*" His eyes brimmed with tears.

Jonas fell on to his hands and knees.

The other boys stirred. They dropped their pebbles and sticks and stared at one another in astonishment.

"Hey, mister?" one of the younger ones said to Nick. "What's going on? What we doing here?"

"Nothing," said Nick. "Go home, the lot of you. Go on, clear off!"

The boys scampered away through the trees, glancing back nervously to make sure that Nick wasn't following them – just a bunch of kids who had been told off for being out too late.

Nick went over to Jonas, who was being sick into a clump of grass. When he finished, he wiped his mouth on his sleeve and tried to stand. Nick helped him to his feet.

Jonas said, "What's been happening, Nick? I thought I was dreaming all this. I had, like, a thing inside me, and it turned me into someone else, and I couldn't make it stop, and—"

"Leave it, Jonas," said Nick. "It's finished. Bad dream's over." He mock-punched Jonas on the shoulder. "Good to have you back. I've been missing you, you know. How you feeling?"

Jonas ran his hand through his hair. "Like my brain's been used as a rugby pitch, but I think I'm going to live."

Nick walked over to Carys, feeling as if they were being wound together on a wire.

Carys's eyes were fuddled and sleepy. "How did I get here?" she said. "Last thing I remember I was catching the bus for Pebbly Beach, then . . . nothing until just now."

"It was Darker," said Nick. "It made you come here."

Carys frowned as she noticed Mr Protheroe. "That's your boss, isn't it?" she said. "What's happened?"

"I don't know, exactly. Mr Protheroe did something and . . . Darker's gone."

"Who's the other boy?"

"My mate Jonas," said Nick. "Darker got him, as well as you."

Nick and Carys approached Mr Protheroe cautiously. His head was bowed.

"Are you all right, Mr Protheroe?" said Nick.

"Helen," Mr Protheroe mumbled. "I did it for Helen. I promised her I would."

Nick said, "Is Helen the girl who was killed in 1963?"

Mr Protheroe looked up. There were tear-tracks on his face. "I was with her when it happened," he said. "We were engaged. The wedding was set for that October, but. . ." He sighed. "I couldn't accept that her death had been an accident. There had to be a reason for it, something behind it all. Everyone else carried on as though Helen had never existed, but I made myself remember. I was the only one who could see what was going on."

"When did you find out about Darker?" said Carys.

"Not for a long time. I only had books to fight it with, you see. I read all I could find about the history of Abernant, and I thought I could see a pattern."

"Every thirty-six years," said Nick.

"Long enough for a new generation to grow up, and for their parents to forget," said Mr Protheroe.

Carys said, "But what was Darker?"

"And how did you get rid of it?" said Nick. "What was that chanting about?"

Mr Protheroe held up his hands in surrender.

"Enough, enough!" he said. "This isn't the time or the place for explanations. Come to the shop tomorrow afternoon, and I'll tell you what I know. Right now, I think it's time we all went home."

23

Next day, Abernant was quiet – even for a
Sunday. Nick walked along the High Street,
thinking, It's gone. No tension, no trouble. Boring
old Abernant again. Nothing ever happens in a
place like this.

Carys was already in Bargain Books when Nick
arrived. Mr Protheroe had carried the chairs in
from the back room, and he and Carys were
drinking tea. A tin of biscuits stood open on the
counter.

"Biscuits, eh?" Nick said to Carys. "You should
feel privileged!"

"We're all privileged!" said Mr Protheroe.
"You're free to help yourself to anything except the
custard creams. How's the arm?"

"Not too bad," said Nick, flexing the fingers of his right hand. "I've got a bruise on my elbow that looks like a tropical sunset, but no serious damage done."

Though he tried to seem cheerful, Nick could see the strain of all that had happened in Mr Protheroe's face. There were shadows under his eyes, and the lines around his mouth had deepened; his hair was more white than grey, and he looked thinner, as though the confrontation with Darker had used him up.

Nick sat down and said, "What did you do last night, Mr Protheroe? Why were you in Porthcwm Woods, anyway? I thought you'd gone to Aberystwyth."

"I did," said Mr Protheroe, "and it was lucky for us that my researches there bore fruit. I found what I wanted in a rare and precious volume – a sixteenth-century grimoire."

"What's one of them?" said Carys.

"A book of spells," said Mr Protheroe. "This particular grimoire was bound in human skin."

Carys made a face.

"The spell I discovered was for the returning of demonic spirits to the place from whence they came," said Mr Protheroe. "The author of the grimoire claimed that he had copied it from an ancient parchment. It was gibberish – dog-Latin and early Welsh, jargon for magicians, I suppose.

But I wrote it down, committed it to memory and returned to Abernant as fast as my car and the speed limit would allow."

"So you performed an exorcism," said Nick.

Mr Protheroe turned up his nose. "I don't care for the term exorcism, Nick," he said. "It smacks of demons and hellfire. What we dealt with in Porthcwm Woods last night was much older than Christianity."

"How much older?" said Carys.

Mr Protheroe set his empty mug on the counter. "I shall attempt to be brief, though after more than thirty years of study, I have some modest claims to be an expert on the subject," he said. "Thousands of years before Christianity arrived, the Celts worshipped rivers and springs, and groves of trees. They believed that such places were the homes of magical beings – spirits."

"The spirits of what?" said Nick.

"The answer to that is long forgotten," said Mr Protheroe. "A few traces of the old beliefs remain – kissing under mistletoe at Christmas, for instance, or throwing a coin into a well and making a wish – but the truths behind the ancient religion were destroyed by the Church.

"In most places, the beliefs died out and the spirits died with them, but I suspect that something found a way of staying alive in Porthcwm Woods, cut off from the rest of time like a fish trapped in a rock pool." Mr Protheroe cocked an eyebrow at Nick. "It was Aspasia Greatorex who clinched it for me. When I read "The Ballad of Tom Dacre", all sorts of things became clear."

Carys said, "There's something I don't get. I know Darker's gone – but where's it gone?"

"I have no idea," said Mr Protheroe. "I don't even know why the spell worked, but I'm glad that it did. Perhaps it dated back to a time when they understood such things, but I can't be sure. It's probably better not to know, like bumblebees."

"Bumblebees?" said Carys.

"According to scientists, it's impossible for bumblebees to fly because they're aerodynamically unsound," said Mr Protheroe. "Fortunately, bumblebees know nothing about the mechanics of flight, and buzz away in blissful ignorance. I suggest that we do the same."

Nick and Carys left the shop, and walked towards the bus stop on Swansea Road.

"How's your friend Jonas?" said Carys.

"I rang his house this morning and talked to his mum. She thinks he's coming down with summer flu and she's going to make him stay in bed for a couple of days."

"D'you think he'll get over what happened?"

"I don't know if any of us ever will."

"Poor Mr Protheroe!" Carys said with a sigh.

"He spent all those years remembering his fiancée. Quite romantic, in a way."

"Not a way I'd like to try," said Nick.

Carys smiled mischievously. "I thought you already were," she said.

"Not any more," said Nick. "I'm over all that now. I'm not going to waste any more time moping over Louise."

Carys punched the air. "Y-ess!" she said. "A breakthrough! Goodbye, Mr Spaniel Eyes, hello, Nick Lloyd!"

"Hello, Carys Bevan," said Nick.

They grinned at each other, and stopped walking.

Nick said, "Is this a relationship?"

"Yes!" said Carys. "We're mates."

"I know, but – I mean, d'you think there's a chance it might change into something else?"

Carys shrugged. "I don't know. Maybe. Why, would it matter?"

Nick thought hard. "Well," he said slowly, "it would matter if it did, but it wouldn't if it didn't. Like, if we were girlfriend-boyfriend kind of thing, that would be all right, and if we stay mates, that'll be all right, too."

"That's perfect then, isn't it?" Carys said.